AN EMPATH'S JOURNEY

BOOK ONE

DAWN M WILLIAMS

This one is for Diana,
who spent days refusing to speak to me
when Journee's life took a turn that she
wasn't expecting. Thank you for reading
it as fast as I could write it.
You really helped me complete this
wonderful story.

NEW ORLEANS

I am so angry that Dad has made us move away from Seattle to New Orleans. Considering that I am so shy, I don't want to have to make new friends when I have had the same girlfriend since preschool. Nicole and I have been inseparable for the last ten years.

Dad is an attorney and is opening a firm in New Orleans where a couple of his college friends are joining him. Dad has always been a criminal attorney and works for the defense. I don't understand why he has decided to make me start my life over now; on my sixteenth birthday no less. He told me yesterday that we were moving! No notice at all! Who does that?

We depart the plane in New Orleans, and I am stunned by the heat. When we left Seattle, the temperature was hovering around thirty-two degrees with chances of a snowstorm and here in Louisiana, it must be close to seventy. November first and I could wear shorts!

I keep the wall up around my mind to block out all of the emotions of those rushing around the terminal as I hurry after Dad to the waiting car. There is a distinct floral smell to the air as we step outside where a limousine is waiting to take us to our new house. The people that are hurrying around the sidewalk have a drawl to their voice that is very soothing. There isn't anything to see outside the airport terminal except for concrete and boring buildings nearby. I was hoping to see palm trees or something tropical.

"You will learn to love it here Journee," Dad tells me once we are seated inside the luxurious car. I have never been inside a limo before, but I can't be excited enough to appreciate the light beige leather, television, full bar, and all the other amenities.

"I already miss Nicole," I grumble as I gaze out the tinted window as the car streams away from the airport. We are taking a major expressway so the only thing I get to see is traffic, businesses, and lower-income neighborhoods. After a couple of minutes, we pass La Salle Park and the thought of walking through nature to soothe my nerves is nearly overwhelming.

There is nothing more to look at until we turn off of the expressway onto St. Charles Avenue and the area improves drastically. There are several restaurants and the appearance of the buildings is much more interesting. This seems to be a big tourist area and I gaze around with interest.

A couple more turns and we are stopping in front of a second empire style mansion made of gray cut stone with balustrades along the first and second floors with iron cresting along the mansard roof. The rectangular windows are flanked by Corinthian columns. The entrance is elevated by several steps leading to arched double doors. Corinthian columns are gracing the front porch. On either side of the house are verandahs flanked by more columns.

I can see behind the house to the right appears to be a school of some sort. There are a lot of large trees everywhere adding a touch of privacy to such a crowded neighborhood.

"I have always told you that you need to try and make new friends." He tells me encouragingly. "Now, you will see how right I am."

Our house in Seattle was a large log cabin set back in the woods and backed up against federal land ensuring we had no close neighbors. Here in New Orleans, it appears that we have moved up in the world as I gaze at the monstrous stone house that I now get to live in. The neighbors are far too close and I am already feeling claustrophobic as he leads me through the arched gate, up the brick walkway, and the many stone steps to the double doors.

We step into a white and gray marble foyer with expensive artwork displayed on the walls as well as antique French furniture and a chandelier. The floor is white and black marble in a triangle design. I am in awe with just the foyer, what does the rest of the house look like?

"Isn't this a little over the top?" I ask Dad sarcastically. "The last I checked we weren't related to royalty."

"Perhaps we should be." He smiles down at me condescendingly. He leads me into the living room, and I gasp at the opulence there. The ceilings are high with elaborate moldings, cream-colored marble walls, a light brown marble fireplace with a beautiful painting of a French countryside mounted above the mantle. The sofa and matching armchairs are also cream-colored velvet with white satin decorative pillows. All of the furniture in the house thus far appears to be French antiques as well as all of the paintings and various other pieces of artwork.

We walk through the kitchen, dining room, morning room, library, study, and even a music room complete with a grand piano and a harp no less. All of the rooms have high ceilings with the elaborate moldings, marble walls, and floors with antique French furniture of various colors and fabrics.

On the third floor is where our bedrooms are, and Dads is black and white. His furniture and floor are black while the walls are a dark gray color and the ceiling and trim are white. His room is more modern than the rest of the house is. He has a bathroom with a Jacuzzi tub, double sinks, and a standup shower.

My bedroom is also French empire like the rest of the house with cream-colored walls and carpet. My bed is a medieval-looking canopy bed with cream-colored lacy bed hangings. My comforter is a pale blue satin and so are my curtains. The bed frame and all of the furniture are pale wood and I even have one of those antique divans or fainting couches. I too have a bathroom with a large sunken garden tub, standup shower, and beautiful marble vanity.

I don't understand how Dad had the time or money to buy us such an expensive new house, completely furnish this new house with all new stuff, and accomplish all of this since yesterday. What is going to happen to everything inside of the log cabin back in Seattle?

"You have enough time for a shower," Dad says as he looks at his watch. "I have a birthday surprise for you and the dress I want you to wear is hanging in the front of your closet."

He disappears with a mysterious smile and closes the door behind him with a soft click. Opening my closet, I see a beautiful light purple satin dress on a hanger. It is strapless with a high waist and stops about three inches above my knee in a full skirt. There are silver high heels on the floor below it and a small velvet bag hung from the hanger. When I open the velvet bag, I find a breathtaking amethyst necklace with matching teardrop earrings.

It is my sixteenth birthday but wearing this new outfit I will look much older. I take a quick shower; dry my long black straight hair and apply some black eyeliner and mascara around my exotically slanted violet eyes and some shiny lip gloss on my full lips. I gaze at my reflection and note my feminine features with a smile of satisfaction. The necklace and earrings bring out the color of my eyes, even though my eyes are quite striking all by themselves.

The older I get the more I realize how much I look like my mother. This saddens me since I lost her to a fever six years ago. She was an empath, just like me, and there are days I wish I could ask for her advice. She taught me how to block out the overload of emotions I get when I am around large crowds of people as well as how to dig into a person's thoughts when I need to find something specific.

It has always been a relief that I am unable to read my dad. I find it peaceful to be in his presence without any efforts to block the bombardment of what he is thinking or feeling. Maybe that is why my mom was attracted to him because of the relaxation of being around him.

I step into the foyer and blush from the look of approval that my dad gives me.

"Oh, Journee!" He whispers emotionally. "You are absolutely breathtaking. You look just like your mother."

"Daddy!" I scold him with a bashful smile. I gaze up at him and wonder what we are doing tonight.

He stands about a foot taller than my dainty five feet and he has a slim athletic build by lifting weights three days a week. He has short medium brown hair that he keeps slightly longer on top than on the sides, so it is spiked. His face is oval with a wide forehead, straight nose, thin lips, and a slight cleft in his chin. Nicole's mom always thought my dad was hot.

He is wearing a black formal suit with a black tie and I can only guess that we are going out for a fancy dinner somewhere to celebrate my birthday. An older woman comes into the foyer and bobs a polite curtsy to us. She is of average height and has gray hair in a neat bob around her ears. Her eyes are a cold blue as they gaze at me as if she is sizing me up. I instantly feel her dislike of me, her arrogance, as well as her fear of my father.

"This is our housekeeper Isadora Vandersteldt." Dad introduces us and I notice her expression warm as she looks at him instead of me. "She will also be doing all the cooking." Her need to please my father is coming off of her in waves and I put up my wall to block out all of the negative energy she is exuding.

"Ms. Vandersteldt, this is my daughter Journee."

"A pleasure to meet you, ma'am." I greet her formally and keep a sweet smile on my face. How could my father think she would make a good housekeeper? It seems she hates me on sight. Her face resumes its chilly expression as she nods her head and looks down her nose at me.

Dad leads me outside to the waiting limousine and I notice a different chauffeur holding the door open for us. He must be close to seven feet tall and has the biggest muscles I have ever seen. He has short blonde hair with a full beard and reminds me of pictures I have seen of Norse Vikings.

"This is James, he is your new driver and bodyguard." Dad stuns me with his introduction.

Bodyguard? Knowing better than to question him with the driver standing right there I just nod at James politely. He never gave me a bodyguard in Seattle!

I slide into the car and wonder at the lack of emotion coming off of James. He wasn't angry, happy, sad, or even mildly curious; just blank.

The car stops in front of a restaurant called Upperline. There are valets at the door to park guest's cars, even though from the outside the restaurant doesn't look all that fancy.

Inside, looks are deceiving and I look around in appreciation as I keep my wall up to block out all of the various emotions going on around me. We are seated in a quiet corner and I take a sip of my water as I look around at the other diners. They are all in formal attire and are speaking softly to each other.

"Why do I need a bodyguard?" I ask him in a tiny voice.

"I will be representing some dangerous people here and I merely want you protected at all times." He explains. "There may come a situation where someone may think they can use you against me. James has protected some very important people in his career."

"I thought maybe you were thinking to protect me from potential boyfriends." I joke with him.

"That won't be necessary." He states without smiling. "If you recall there will be no boyfriends until college."

"I was teasing Daddy." I look away from him in disappointment. He, of course, ignores my attempt at a joke.

The waiter comes to take our order and as usual, I am not allowed to give my opinion on what I eat. He orders a Taste of New Orleans dinner that comes with Gumbo, turtle soup, duck etouffee, fried green tomatoes with shrimp remoulade, spicy shrimp with cornbread, and slow-roasted duckling.

I always feel bad when Dad orders more than a one-course meal because I am forced to nibble on all the food that arrives at the table until I feel ill. To my surprise, the waiter brings an expensive bottle of champagne and even pours me a glass. I raise my eyebrow at Dad over my glass, wondering if the waiter made a mistake assuming I was over twenty-one.

"My parents allowed me to drink champagne when I was your age on special occasions," Dad says once the waiter has disappeared. "You are a young woman now."

He raises his glass and I pick mine up as he smiles at me.

"To my little girl all grown up into a beautiful woman." He toasts before clinking my glass and watching me take a sip at the same time that he does.

I have to admit that I don't care for the taste of the champagne. It isn't sweet enough and leaves a dry feeling in my mouth. I hide my distaste from Dad however and smile at him brightly, so he thinks I appreciate his gesture.

"You will be going to a private Catholic school here as well," Dad explains to me. "De La Salle High School is one of the best in the city and I thought it would be easier for you to fit in since you always attended Catholic up in Seattle."

"Do we need to get uniforms?" I ask curiously.

"They are already in your closet." He replies. "On the other side from where your dress was hung. I will be working some long hours for a while as I get my office established downtown. James will take you to and from school each day and under no circumstances are you allowed to leave campus without him. Ms. Vandersteldt will be at the house each afternoon when you get home from school should you need anything."

The waiter starts to bring our food and I have to admit I love the Cajun-style food here. It's spicy but not overly so and the taste is heavenly.

We eat in companionable silence, each lost in our thoughts; no doubt about our recent move. As I eat, I look curiously at the people that are sitting around the restaurant. Being an empath, even though I block out the overload, I am still drawn to watch people and notice their body language and facial expressions. I have learned that by paying attention to these things I can tell what they are feeling or if they are lying without using my empathy.

I don't think most people even know how to read someone's facial expressions or body language, but after paying attention for so many years I have learned what even the smallest muscle movement can mean. It has helped me so that I can keep myself tuned out from their emotions and not be so overwhelmed.

There is a young couple not too far from our table that has caught my attention. They look like they are in their middle twenties and their dress and mannerisms tell me they fit right in socially.

The woman is picture-perfect with every golden blonde hair in place, but her demeanor tells me that she wishes to be anywhere but here. Her wan facial expression tells me that she fears the man she is with and is attempting to hide this from him. If he moves his arm too quickly, she flinches just enough for my trained eye to notice, but most likely not his.

Too inquisitive to help myself, I open up to just this couple and am instantly taken aback by the man's egotistical arrogance. He is positive that the woman with him is only there to serve and please him. The restrained violence coming off of him nearly makes me feel sick to my stomach.

The woman's terror is so palpable it nearly knocks me out of my chair. She is relieved to be in public because he won't hurt her here, but she is terrified to leave because the anticipation of what he will do later is almost more than she can bear.

It is this part of my gift that makes me angry because there is nothing that I can do to help this poor woman. She will most likely never leave him, even if the opportunity presents itself to her.

I sip my champagne slowly even though I don't like it because Dad thinks he is doing something special for me and I don't wish to hurt his feelings. I eat a few bites of each course that is brought to the table, hoping to have room for when dessert is finally brought out.

I have to admit that I am not thrilled about trying the turtle soup, but after I sip a spoonful hesitantly and am surprised that it is pretty good. Dad seems to have quite the appetite as he nearly finishes each course. He has such a high metabolism that everything that he eats just gets burned up.

I, on the other hand, eat like a bird and if I am stressed at all my appetite is the first to go. I am not even a hundred pounds and stand at barely five feet tall with a petite frame. It doesn't take much food to satisfy my hunger usually.

Dad sits back with a happy sigh after our dessert plates are cleared away.

"How did you like the Cajun food?" He asks me curiously.

"I liked it," I confess with a warm smile. "It had just the right amount of spice and the flavors were spectacular."

"You didn't like the champagne." He states. I shake my head, sad that I disappointed him.

"I didn't like the way it dried out my mouth and I guess I wanted it to be sweeter," I confess.

"I know what to have you try next time." He tells me with a smile. "You would probably enjoy a sweet white wine or maybe a blush wine."

He stands up and politely pulls out my chair and I notice after I stand that the young couple I was watching is leaving at the same time. The woman's face has paled to a nearly gray color as she meekly follows the man from the dining room. She has her bottom lip pulled between her teeth and is biting it anxiously.

Dad and I follow them out to the curb where they are waiting for the valet to fetch their car. The man is whispering in her ear and to everyone else, it appears that he is just being romantic, but I can see from his body language he is furious with her about something. She is standing completely still and even though her facial expression is carefully blank I can feel her terror coming off of her in waves. I desperately want to help her, but I am only a sixteen-year-old girl and am much smaller than her, no help against the much larger man.

Dad leads me past them and into our limousine that has just pulled up to the curb. James keeps himself between me and the other people on the sidewalk as he carefully looks the area over for danger.

DADDY, NO!

"Sasha." I am jolted awake by my dad whispering in my ear as he lies against me, effectively pinning me to the bed. I try to squirm out from under him, but he is like a dead weight against me.

"Daddy?" I whimper, unable to draw a deep breath to call out any louder. He doesn't seem to hear me as he continues to whisper my mother's name in my ear. I can hear the pain lacing his voice as he pins me beneath him and strokes my hair softly.

I can't move and need to conserve my breath for breathing purposes instead of yelling like I want to do. Tears trickle down my cheeks into my hair as I wish that I could use my empath abilities to get a reading on what he is feeling but I have never been able to do that with him.

He is acting like he is sleepwalking, and I know that you aren't supposed to wake up someone who is doing that. I lie still and hope that he will either fall asleep or get up and go back to his room. Unfortunately, he is under the covers with me and I can feel that he is only wearing a pair of boxers against my short nightgown.

I never expected the fact that looking so much like my mother would have this effect on Dad. I feel intense compassion for him as he kisses my temple and continues to murmur Mom's name into my hair.

Eventually, he gets up and leaves my room walking as if he is in a trance. Tears begin to flow now that I am alone, and I am not sure if it is because I miss Mom or because of the reaction to Dad.

My alarm goes off and I groan as I turn it off and trudge into the bathroom for a shower. I leave the water on the cool side and by the time I am done I am slightly more awake. It feels as if I didn't get any sleep at all as I put on one of my new uniforms and grimace as I look at myself in the mirror. The skirt is a dark gray color, the blazer is maroon, and I am wearing black tights to go along with my black flats.

I have left my long black hair hanging loose around my waist and I put on some light eyeliner, mascara, and lip gloss. My violet eyes are more pronounced due to the dark circles under my eyes.

Gathering up my school bag I make my way down to the foyer where James is waiting for me. I follow him out to the limousine and am grateful that he doesn't speak to me. He holds open the door for me and closes it gently after I slide into the back seat. The ride to school is too quick and before I am prepared James is holding the door open for me in front of the school. The school is your typical brick building with nothing out of the ordinary.

"It is always better than what you imagine it to be," James says to me in a soft voice as I stand there looking at the school nervously.

"Really?" I ask in a tiny voice, just wanting to turn around and have him take me back home.

"Really." He smiles down at me encouragingly. "Just make sure you smile back at people and if someone talks to you it's always good to allow a conversation to start."

"Ok." I nod at him as I take a step towards the school. "Thanks."

As I head towards the front doors, I notice that my limousine has drawn some curious stares as I make my way inside. The building is a two-story brick building with a large cross right next to the double doors leading to the office.

The receptionist has my schedule waiting for me as well as a small map to help me find my way around. The name on my schedule gives me pause, however; Francesca Lambrix.

"I'm sorry ma'am, but I think you gave me the wrong schedule." I hand it back to her with a polite smile.

"Your father explained that he registered you under his mother's name for your protection." The receptionist explains to me. "All of the teachers have received a memo to this effect. You may have everyone call you by your real first name if you wish."

The hallways are fairly empty since I am a little early to find my locker and classrooms. My locker is in the sophomore hallway on the second floor and I manage the combination to the lock without a problem.

I take a couple of minutes to look at the map concerning where my locker is so that I can locate all of my classes from here. My first-hour class is just down the hallway and it looks like my other six classrooms will be easy to find as well.

The hallways are starting to become congested and I look around curiously as students gather in groups to talk, rush through the hallways, or stop at their lockers. I make a short stop in the bathroom to check my appearance and satisfied that I look alright I head down the hallway to my first class.

My first hour-class is English, and my teacher's name is Alice Fitzgerald and she is a tiny little old lady with silver hair and a bright smile. She puts me at ease instantly, agreeing to call me Journee instead of what my schedule says. She tells me where to sit and I fall in love with her Irish accent.

I walk back to my desk and smile back at a couple of girls as I pass them. My desk is almost at the back of the room, for which I am grateful, where I can watch everyone else instead of being the center of attention.

A dark-haired girl with big brown eyes sits down in front of me and turns to me with a welcoming smile. She is breathtakingly beautiful with seductive facial features and long layered hair that frames her face.

"Hi. I'm Victoria." She introduces herself. "Where are you from?"

"My name is Journee. I moved here from Seattle." I smile back at her bashfully.

"So, what brings you to New Orleans?" She asks.

"My dad is an attorney and decided to open a practice here with some college classmates," I explain with a sigh. "Every sophomore wants to start over in a new school partway through the school year, right?"

I nonchalantly allow myself to get a reading from her and am thrilled to see that she is sincerely curious about me and is hopeful that she can get to know me. I only get good vibes from her and know from just those few seconds that she is someone I can trust.

"What about your mom?" She asks, her expression hesitant.

"She died when I was ten," I explain without looking sad, not wanting to make her uncomfortable.

"Is it just you and your dad then?" She continues to probe. "No siblings?"

"Just me and my dad. What about you?" I take charge of the questions with a grin.

"I have an older brother named Rafe who is a senior this year." She grins back at me. "My mom stays at home and is involved in charities and some historical societies and my dad is an FBI agent."

Before I can ask anything, further Mrs. Fitzgerald calls the class to order and after handing me a copy of *The Merchant of Venice*, she has everyone open up to the second chapter. Thankfully, my school in Seattle already covered this book at the beginning of the year so this will all be review for me.

After the bell rings Victoria and I walk out into the hall together and she snatches my class schedule from me and is excited to see that we have all of the same classes.

"Why is your schedule for someone named Francesca?" Victoria asks.

"I guess Dad doesn't want anyone to know I am registered here. He seems to think I am in danger or something." I explain to her uncomfortably.

Our next class is algebra 2 and my teacher is Ms. Karla Anderson. She is probably in her early thirties with blonde hair she keeps in a bun on the back of her head. If I were to guess her heritage, I would guess Scandinavian. She looks like she will be a strict teacher due to the closed expression on her face.

After algebra is chemistry and then advanced placement world history. I am pleased to note that I am not behind in any of my classes so far and my transition should be a smooth one.

Victoria and I make our way to the lunchroom after our history class and we meet up with another of her friends I haven't met yet, Clare. Clare is about five inches taller than my five feet with golden blonde hair, blue eyes, and the perfect build for a cheerleader. She gives me a friendly smile and I can feel the positive energy from her.

Victoria and I are standing in line waiting to order cheeseburgers when a tall guy with dark hair steps up to Victoria. He has a teasing expression on his face as he pokes her in the back of the head lightly. He must be a couple of inches taller than six feet with broad shoulders and looks like he could play football. His face is oval with a naturally golden complexion and a pair of striking gray eyes. His nose is bold above full lips surrounded by a light goatee.

He looks over at me curiously and when I reach out to get a reading on him, I am stunned to feel that he is doing the same thing to me. Other than my mother, I have never met another empath before.

I drop my gaze uncomfortably as I wonder if he knows what I am as well.

"Who is your friend Victoria?" He asks, his voice deep and husky with a slight southern drawl.

"This is Journee Parisi." Victoria tells him, completely missing the tension between the two of us. "She just moved here from Seattle with her dad. Journee this is my older brother Rafe."

"Your new friend is just like me and Grams," Rafe whispers so only Victoria and I can hear. Victoria gives me a look of stunned surprise before she looks up at her brother.

"Are you sure?" She asks in amazement.

"Yes." He chuckles. "You could say we bumped into each other."

"So, she is an empath like you?" Victoria whispers as she continues to look at me as if she is thrilled with the news.

I nod my head at the same time that Rafe does.

"I have never met someone other than family who is like me," I state as I look up at Rafe curiously and am instantly snared in those gorgeous eyes of his. He appears just as interested in me which makes me blush and look over at Victoria.

"You aren't gifted?" I ask her quietly. Victoria shakes her head.

"Thankfully no." Victoria laughs. "I like the mystery of not knowing what is going on in someone's head."

Victoria finally notices the way her brother and I are looking at each other and she punches Rafe in the arm with a grin.

"Oh! Well well!" Victoria chants tauntingly. "Look who likes each other!"

"Stop it, Vic." Rafe scolds her as he notices my discomfort. "You are going to chase away your new friend."

"My dad would never let me date anyone before college anyway," I state in a tiny voice, my disappointment is evident.

"Oh, that's an easy one to hide." Victoria states with a wave of her hand. "You are my new friend and he just happens to be my older brother who has absolutely no interest in you anyway because he is a stuck-up jerk."

Rafe laughs and Victoria joins in with a naughty grin on her face.

"Leave it to my baby sister to have a natural ability to misbehave," Rafe states as we grab our cheeseburgers and head to a table.

Victoria insists that I sit across from her next to Rafe and I color a bright pink when he gives me an intense gaze which makes me bashfully look away.

I can eat part of my burger after Rafe turns his attention to his lunch while Victoria fills me in on everything De La Salle.

"So where do you and your dad live?" Victoria asks.

"2300 block of Prytania Street in the garden district," I tell her as I try to remember the exact address. "My dad bought this huge stone house that looks like a mini castle from the outside. I think it's way over the top. I miss our log cabin back in Washington. Are you guys anywhere close by?"

"We should be just a couple blocks north of you on First Street," Rafe informs me with a smile. "I think I know which house you are talking about. I don't remember it being for sale though."

"That's awesome!" Victoria exclaims. "We can walk to each other's houses!"

"So, what does your dad do?" Rafe asks, stealing the conversation away from his sister.

"He is an attorney." I fill him in around a bite of my food. "He is opening a practice here with a couple of guys he went to college with."

"What kind of law does he practice?" He wants to know.

"He is a defense attorney. He likes to fight for the underdog he says." I share with a laugh.

"So, who in your family is like you?" Victoria asks bluntly as she watches my interaction with Rafe avidly.

"My mom was," I tell her sadly. "I wish she was still here so I could ask questions sometimes. My dad doesn't know anything about it and Mom always told me to never tell him."

"Can't you tell by getting a reading off of him whether or not he would accept your gift?" Victoria asks curiously.

"I have never been able to read him," I state with a shrug and I am surprised by the shocked look on Rafe's face. "Isn't that normal?" I ask him curiously.

"I have never run across someone that I was unable to get a feeling from," Rafe says thoughtfully. "I can ask my grams about it; she may know why."

"I just thought it had something to do with him being my dad." I look at Rafe intently. "I would love to hear what your grams has to say about it."

"She owns a new age shop in the French quarter," Victoria explains. "If you can come over to our house one day soon, we can bring you over there and introduce you."

"New age; like fortune-telling and stuff?" I question in surprise.

"Yep." Victoria laughs at my expression. "She has visions; especially when she touches people or objects."

"Do you know any of your mother's family?" Rafe asks curiously.

"No." I shake my head. "She would never talk about her past before she met my dad. He said she grew up down here in Louisiana somewhere. Why?"

"Your gift probably goes through your mom's side of the family," Rafe explains. "You miss your mom and wish she were here to answer questions. What if her mom or a sibling is gifted and lives nearby? Wouldn't you like to meet them?"

"I don't understand how I am supposed to find them. My dad knows nothing more than I do and Mom didn't leave any clues behind." I respond as we get up and head out of the cafeteria.

"Haven't you seen all those advertisements for the at-home DNA kits where you can connect with family members?" He questions incredulously.

"I don't think my dad would want me to do that." I hedge, my gut telling me that Dad would freak out a little.

"We don't need to tell him anything," Rafe says encouragingly. "I think it's important for you to find a gifted family that you can use for support. Let me take care of everything for you, alright?"

"Are you sure?" I exclaim. "I don't want to burden you with this."

"You aren't a burden Journee," Rafe whispers into my ear, his husky drawl making me blush as I nod my agreement.

"You have to be a secret Rafe," I whisper back before he moves away.

"I won't get you into trouble." He nuzzles my ear. "Trust me."

I look up into his amazingly seductive gray eyes and smile timidly as I nod my head. Rafe gently probes my mind and I can feel the question in his touch before he tries to read me. I permit him by allowing myself to use my gift on him. It is a strange feeling having someone do the same thing to me that I have done to others. The first thing I feel is Rafe's sincerity and his compassion for others. He is honest, loyal, and protective of those that he loves. At the very forefront of his thoughts, I feel his excitement at finding me, another empath that he is attracted to. His need to get to know me is a real boost to my low self-esteem.

He kisses my cheek tenderly before he hurries away down the hallway leaving Victoria gazing at me with wonder on her face.

"I was beginning to think my brother would never find a girlfriend." She says as she looks at me with awe. "My parents are going to love you."

"I'm sure he felt like I did," I explain to her. "I never went out with anyone because I am too different. I wanted someone I could share my ability with."

THE NEW BODYGUARD

I bring home a couple of snacks from the cafeteria so that I won't have to face our new housekeeper. Ms. Vandersteldt is way too intimidating for someone like me. I hate confrontation and the way she glared at me yesterday just makes me cringe at the thought.

James is standing by the back door of the limousine when I walk up, and he raises his eyebrow at me questioningly before I get in.

"You were right." I chuckle. "It was much easier than I expected, and you will be happy to know I even made a couple of friends."

"Way to go Journee." He praises me with a sincere smile. I blush and grin happily as I slide into the back seat.

The ride home is too quick and before I am ready the front door looms in front of me. James is waiting behind me and seems to notice my hesitation, so he steps around me to hold open the door for me.

I take a deep breath for strength and step inside praying that the housekeeper is nowhere in sight but groan inwardly because she appears to be waiting for me in the foyer.

"Will you be requiring a snack this afternoon?" She asks, her tone icy and disdainful.

Before I can utter a peep, James towers over Ms. Vandersteldt with a glare.

"You had better adjust your tone, old woman," James states in deceptively soft tones. "This is Journee's house, not yours, and if she feels like having something to eat, she will help herself to *her* kitchen. If you wish to keep your position here, I suggest you find your humility because you are just a servant."

Ms. Vandersteldt's face pales to a sickly gray color and she looks instantly afraid before she turns on her heel to hurry out of the foyer.

"Thank you, James," I whisper sincerely.

"No problem kiddo." He chuckles. "I don't like her anyway and someone had to put her in her place. Let's go have brownies and ice cream while they are fresh from the oven." James suggests enthusiastically, just like a little kid.

I nod and follow him to the kitchen where a steaming pan of brownies is cooling on the counter. He grabs the ice cream from the freezer while I put some brownies in a couple of bowls and grab some spoons. James scoops us some ice cream on top of the brownies before heating some fudge in the microwave to layer on the top. Before he lets me take my bowl, he sprays whipped cream on top and gestures for me to follow him.

He takes me to the back yard where there is a small patio table set up in the middle of the garden. I can't believe the number of flowering plants down here in November. There are sculptures, birdbaths, fountains, arbors with climbing flowers, and even a small pond.

"I still can't believe the climate difference here," I state as I sit down across from my new bodyguard. "It was snowing when we left Seattle yesterday."

"Winter's here are great," James says between bites of his dessert. "Last winter I was in Canada. Talk about snow and cold."

James fills me in on his last assignment working for a Canadian diplomat while we eat. It still surprises me that my dad thinks I need a bodyguard. I am relieved that James turned out to be such a nice guy. I didn't expect him to stick up for me in front of the housekeeper like he did.

I rinse and load our dishes into the dishwasher before heading up to my room to get started on my homework. Even though I am not behind in any of my classes I still have a lot of homework to do before tomorrow.

I start with the Shakespeare book, read the first four chapters of the book, and take notes so that I understand what is being said. Moving on to Algebra I work on the three pages of problems that are due by the second hour tomorrow morning. Unfortunately, I am not good at math and my dad usually helps me, but with his new practice, I think I will have to struggle through it alone.

It is well after dark by the time I finally finish my math and I stand up to stretch out the stiffness in my back.

"Come in," I call out at the knock on my door and smile at James when he steps inside.

"Are you planning on eating dinner?" He asks as he gives my cluttered desk a pointed look.

"I probably should but I still have four classes of homework to do tonight," I explain to him with a sigh.

"You look stressed." James points out logically. "Come take a small break and eat something. You are way too tiny to skip meals."

I nod and follow him down to the dining room and frown when I see that Dad hasn't come home from work yet.

"I made steaks on the grill if you want to just eat in the kitchen," James suggests.

"Where is Ms. Vandersteldt?" I ask curiously.

"Your dad fired her," James states with a shrug.

"You told him to, didn't you?" I ask him in surprise.

"Yep." He grins at me. "I am a pretty good cook and I suggested to your dad to have a cleaning service come in once a week instead."

A bright smile lights up my face at the load off my shoulders that I don't have to stress over interacting with that awful woman anymore.

He has set the small kitchen table for the two of us and it looks rather cozy. He made small sizzler steaks with baked sweet potatoes, steamed broccoli, and garlic bread. My stomach growls loudly when I get a whiff of the food.

"Dig in girl," James orders me with a grin as he sits down across from me before he pops a large slice of steak into his mouth with a moan of pleasure. The steak is a perfectly cooked medium rare and the sweet potato has butter and some kind of a caramelized glaze that is scrumptious. He has sprinkled shredded cheese over the broccoli, and I think he made the garlic bread himself.

I manage to eat almost everything on my plate due to my complete relaxation around James. Sitting back with a sigh I smile at him happily.

"That was awesome! Thank you." I tell him. "I didn't realize I was hungry until I smelled it all."

"It was pretty good wasn't it?" He says confidently. "Did you need any help with your homework?"

Instinctively, I peek into his mind and see that he is good at math.

"I wished I had known you were good at math. I would have had you help me with it." I blurt without thinking.

"Yep. It was my favorite subject." He replies without missing a beat.

"Good. Starting tomorrow you are my new math tutor too." I inform him with relief. I clean up the kitchen before heading back upstairs to my homework.

I manage to finish up my chemistry, history, religion, and Latin homework before nine o'clock. After packing up my homework into my school bag I wander around to look for James and let him know I am going to retire for the night.

I find my dad in the kitchen eating a steak dinner that James must have prepared for him while they are chatting.

"Hey princess!" Dad greets me with a warm smile. "James tells me that you had a good first day of school."

"I did. How was your first day?" I ask him after giving him a big hug and kissing his cheek.

"It was productive." He tells me with a sigh. "It will be at least another week before we can start seeing clients."

"I made a friend today," I state softly as I look at Dad hesitantly. "I was hoping I could go to her house this weekend."

"I would need to meet her parents first," Dad replies as he gazes at me intently.

"I'm sure that can be arranged," I tell him hopefully. "Do you think maybe you take a few minutes to meet them tomorrow?"

My heart is racing as I hope he is not thinking that I am being pushy or asking for too much when he is so busy with his new practice.

"I can take some time tomorrow so that you might be able to spend the weekend with your new friend," Dad replies with a long-suffering sigh as if he is so put out, and then grins at me. "Just text me tomorrow and let me know what time and where."

"Yay!" I squeal and rush up to my room to text Victoria. Flopping down on my bed I send a quick message to my new friend explaining what my dad wants and if he can meet her parents tomorrow. I am thrilled when she texts me back just a few minutes later asking if my dad can meet her parent's for coffee at Café du Monde in the quarter tomorrow morning at nine. Hurrying back down to the kitchen I rush in and wait for James and Dad to stop talking.

"Tomorrow morning at nine o'clock at the Cafe du Monde in the quarter?" I ask him eagerly. He nods at me with a smile.

"What are their names?" He asks.

"Dimitri and Monique Antonescu." I gush happily. "Good night!"

I practically float up to my room I am so happy that I might get to spend the weekend with Victoria and Rafe. Just the thought of seeing Rafe again makes me want to scream from the rooftops. He is so hot!

Once again, I am jarred from sleep by my dad as he lies over me moaning my mother's name as he moves his hands over me everywhere. I whimper, too afraid to wake him up and risk the trauma he may face at finding himself in my bed. I can't stop myself from struggling valiantly when he slams his mouth down on mine with a groan only to have him pin me effortlessly beneath him. Just when I think he is going to go too far he suddenly stops, and he is out of my bedroom before I realize I am free.

Rushing to the bathroom, I vomit until I dry heave and then brush my teeth for a long time before gargling with mouthwash. Too afraid to get back in bed I curl up on the fainting couch and rock myself soothingly for what feels like hours.

My alarm goes off and it feels like I just fell asleep. I take a shower and get ready quickly before heading downstairs to meet James. He is not in the foyer, so I walk back to the kitchen to see if he is still in there.

James is in there and hands me a one-egg omelet with feta cheese, mushrooms, tomatoes, and hollandaise sauce on the top. There is a slice of dark pumpernickel toast next to my eggs and a glass of orange juice for me at the small table.

"I'm not all that hungry." I try to give it back to him.

"You didn't eat breakfast yesterday either." James raises his eyebrow at me knowingly. "Sit down and eat some. We have plenty of time."

I sit down with a sigh and manage to eat more than I expected considering how stressed I am right now. James joins me and has no problem inhaling his.

"I know the real reason you are so excited to go and spend the weekend with Victoria." He states as he pushes his plate away.

I can't help but pale at his announcement as I try to act nonchalant.

"I don't know what you are talking about," I state airily as I wave my hand in front of my face. James laughs at me.

"Your dad left for his office over an hour ago to make time for the Antonescu's," James explains to me, now serious. "Part of my job as your bodyguard is to know everything about the person I am protecting. I saw you with Rafe yesterday and I am aware of your father's rule that he doesn't want you to date until you are done with high school too."

A tear trickles down my face at the unfairness of having my happiness crushed. Pushing away my plate I rise from the table and move to leave the kitchen.

"Sit down Journee," James says in that soft voice of his. Sighing sadly, I sit back down and hang my head, waiting for him to tell me how he will tell Dad what he knows.

"It isn't part of my job description to tattle to your father and it isn't any of my business if you follow those rules or not," James tells me. "I am here to protect you from harm. It was my job to have the Antonescu family screened and you will be pleased to hear that I will not stand in the way of your budding relationship with Rafe, nor will I be saying anything to your father, Ansen."

I raise my eyes to his in disbelief. He is smiling at me as it hits me that he isn't going to tell Dad about Rafe. I use my gift on him again and hear how impressed he is with Rafe.

"I don't understand," I whisper confused. "You aren't going to tell my dad because you are impressed with Rafe?"

"I was not hired to make sure you are an obedient daughter Journee. What I found out about Rafe impressed me. He is a great kid, and no one has a negative word to say about him. He is starting college in the fall and is going into law enforcement; just like his father. As far as I could find out he has never dated anyone seriously before he met you."

"Thank you, James." I state sincerely.

I clean up the kitchen before we head to school. Victoria is waiting for me on the front steps and her eyes practically bug out of her head when she sees the limo.

"What's up with this?" She asks, obviously impressed.

"My dad hired me a bodyguard." I shrug uncomfortably. "He thinks his job puts me in danger. Victoria, this is James."

"Didn't I see you by the office yesterday?" Victoria asks him pointedly.

"Indeed, you did." James smiles at her warmly. "I was assuring my girl's safety."

"You aren't spending the weekend at my house, are you?" Victoria asks as she puts her hand on her hip with an attitude.

"That will not be necessary, however, I will be close by." James nods at her formally. "I will be back after school Journee."

"Thanks, James." I smile at him affectionately.

Rafe is waiting for me just inside the front door and gives me a smile that instantly makes me blush.

"What's with the limo?" He asks. "Was that your dad?"

"That is her bodyguard with her personal limousine," Victoria states dramatically. "Her dad thinks his job puts her in danger."

"With that logic, we both should have our bodyguards because of Dad being an FBI agent." Rafe laughs.

As we walk down the hallway towards the stairs Rafe grabs my hand in his and gives it a gentle squeeze.

"So, our parents are meeting your dad for coffee," Rafe says, his deep voice giving me goosebumps. "When do we find out if you get to come to spend the weekend?"

"Dad knows I am excited so I am sure he will text me as soon as he decides. Otherwise, I will be begging him by nine-thirty." I reply as I stroke my thumb across the back of his hand.

HEATH THE CREEP

Victoria and I are in our third-hour chemistry class when Dad finally texts me to let me know that I can spend the weekend with the Antonescu's. He explains that James will bring me home so I can pack a bag before driving me over to Victoria's house. I am to keep James' number handy just in case I might need him because he will be at home on call.

Victoria and I have a hard time paying attention after that and are sternly lectured by Mr. Walker, our chemistry teacher three times before the bell rings. Rafe is waiting for us when we step out into the hallway and I nod at him with an inhibited smile.

I feel a rush of jealousy come over me as Rafe and I gaze into each other's eyes because I look up to see a red-headed girl staring at us hatefully. I instinctively grab Rafe's hand and peek into her head and am astounded at the depths of the hatred she feels for me.

I gasp at the intensity and can tell that Rafe is feeling this too.

"That is Kristin," Rafe whispers softly into my ear. "I went out on one date with her last year and she just never got over it."

A rush of compassion comes over me because I can tell by her appearance that she doesn't have any friends. Her hair is naturally curly but instead of keeping it gelled she lets it frizz all around her face. She has severe acne with an oily sheen all over her skin. To top it all off, she wears thick plastic-rimmed glasses and has braces. Poor girl.

We turn away and head down the hall towards our next class with Rafe holding my hand while Victoria and I discuss what trouble we can get into this weekend.

Rafe misses lunch with us because he has a meeting with the basketball team that he cannot miss. Victoria and I are in line waiting to buy a slice of pizza when a guy with light brown hair steps up behind me.

"Hey, gorgeous." He says in an arrogant voice. "I'm Heath."

I look back at him as he towers over me standing too close. I try to back up a step but end up stepping on Victoria instead. He must be an inch or two taller than Rafe and is just as muscular, it is obvious that he plays sports too. He has a square face with a nose that is a touch too wide for his face, full lips, brown eyes, and a slight cleft in his strong jaw. He is very cute but also knows it and plays it to his advantage. His body language and facial expression alone tell me that all he wants from me is to get into my pants without my purposely reading him. I instantly block the visual going on in his head as well as his thought when he caught sight of me.

"Hello," I reply so that I am not being rude and arch my eyebrow at him haughtily. His smile turns seductive as he leans so close, he is rubbing against the front of my blazer.

"How about we go to the game tonight?" He asks. "New girl like you, I can show you around." Boldly, he looks me up and down and when he moves to lean even closer, I place both my hands on his chest and shove upward, pushing up with my legs and taking him unawares.

"Get off me!" I exclaim and before Heath can even gain his footing James is there pulling him away from me.

"Journee are you alright?" James asks without looking at me.

"I'm fine," I reply, surprised he was close enough to protect me. The whole cafeteria has gathered to see what is going on as Victoria pulls me back alongside her and wraps an arm protectively around my shoulders.

"You heard her!" James says to Heath in his soft voice. "She isn't interested so take your punk ass somewhere else."

Heath glares daggers at me before he saunters away as if he wasn't just humiliated by my bodyguard. I can hear everyone wondering who James is and why he suddenly appeared out of nowhere to protect me. Victoria whispers to Clare, one of her friends, that James is my bodyguard and soon the whole cafeteria is buzzing about it.

I just want to disappear, but I hold my head high and refuse to be the bashful girl that prayed to be invisible anymore.

"Nice push," James tells me proudly. "Who showed you how to do that?"

"Dad." I smile at him. "He told me pushing upwards like that makes them off balance because they aren't expecting the force to come from that direction."

"It might be a good idea for me to show you some more self-defense moves." James nods at me. "Enjoy your lunch kiddo."

James disappears through the crowd and I get to listen to a ton of girls tell me how awesome it was to have Heath the Creep put in his place. A couple of the girls even whisper to me that they went out with him only to have him force himself on them. His family is some wealthy New Orleans founding family or something so the girl that tried to press charges was paid for her silence. Nice.

I have instantly attained popularity status as a result. Rafe joins us when our lunch hour is nearly over and has already heard about what happened before he left the gym. He wants to go pound on Heath because it is already known that I am Rafe's girl and Heath stepped over the line by asking me out. I convince him that violence is never the answer and Rafe agrees to leave Heath alone for the time being.

Victoria and I don't pay attention in the rest of our classes and are scolded several times by the time school are finally over for the weekend. Unfortunately, Kristin is in a couple of my afternoon classes and she continues to glare hatefully at me the entire time. I tried smiling at her but after she looked like she wanted to kill me I opted for just ignoring her.

I pass Heath in the hallway and it is obvious from the expression on his face that he is not finished with me yet. I refuse to look at him and just keep my gift open to him just for safety's sake. It frightens me when I feel how he thinks he is untouchable and can do as he pleases and take what he wants from whomever he pleases without suffering consequences.

James opens the door for me when I walk up, and he winks at me before closing the door. I am surprised when he follows me up to my room and sits down on my bed while I start to pack my overnight bag.

"What's up?" I ask him hesitantly. James sighs and looks away from me uncomfortably for a second.

"I feel like your father all of a sudden." He states quietly. "I know Rafe is your first boyfriend and I also know that you are a good girl and have no intentions of anything happening this weekend, but sometimes the heat of the moment can get away from us."

"James!" I exclaim, horrified at what he is trying to tell me.

"Journee, just listen to me." He pleads sincerely. I feel his genuine worry for me that I may get in over my head this weekend and have to deal with something unexpected. His deep affection for me surprises me since we have only known each other for a couple of days, but his feelings for me are strong and very paternal.

"I won't get in over my head this weekend, I promise!" I exclaim, just wanting to avoid this uncomfortable conversation.

"You are a very sensitive girl and I know that you are excited about your new relationship with Rafe. I just want you to take it slow with him and not let kissing lead to something you aren't ready for. Sex is better after you develop strong feelings for someone because it is an expression of those feelings. Right now, it would just be awkward fumbling and disappointment." James tells me earnestly.

"I promise," I vow to him sincerely. "I don't think you are supposed to protect my virtue." I joke with him, trying to lighten the mood.

"Your innocence is a very important part of your sweet nature little one," James says he taps my nose affectionately before he walks to the door. "I will be downstairs in the foyer."

After he closes the door behind himself, I stare at it in amazement. I honestly thought having a bodyguard pestering me all the time was going to be a pain in my side, not having affection for the big brute or the fact that he is quickly becoming an important part of my life.

I change out of my school uniform and put on a pair of light blue skinny jeans and a pale purple cashmere sweater. Slipping on a pair of brown leather flats and grabbing a jacket, I head down to the foyer where James is pacing back and forth.

I can feel his agitation and know that he is worried about me.

"I promised," I whisper, feeling bad for his anxiety. James looks up at me and smiles.

"I know." He whispers back.

"Not that it is a bad thing, but are you supposed to allow yourself to become so attached to me?" I ask him curiously.

"No. Rule number one." He recites with a grimace. I step up to him and give him a big hug and pull his face down so I can kiss his cheek.

"Well, I am getting attached to you too, *Uncle James*," I say in a sassy tone of voice.

"Come on brat." He ruffles my hair before opening the front door for me.

He pulls into Victoria's driveway and opens my door for me while gazing at me intensely.

"I'm a good girl remember?" I ask him as I raise my eyebrow at him teasingly.

"Yes, you are Journee." He says with a sigh. "You can text me for anything, even if it's just to go buy you guys pizza and ice cream. Even though I am not technically on duty this weekend I would appreciate it if you would text me and let me know if you go anywhere. Just in case."

"I will be happy to if not to just put you at ease," I reply solemnly.

I skip up the steps to the large yellow and white house with blue trim with a happy smile on my face. Victoria rips the door open before I can even knock, and I turn around to wave at James before following her inside the house.

I fall in love with her house instantly because it is so cozy and family-friendly. There is no marble anywhere and it reminds me of what our log cabin looked like before Mom died.

A beautiful woman with strawberry blonde hair, light blue eyes, and porcelain skin steps up to me with a welcoming smile.

"Welcome Journee!" She says as she gives me a warm hug. "I'm Victoria's mom, Monique. How about you girls come into the kitchen I have a pan of apple crisp that is still warm with some ice cream."

I didn't expect Rafe and Victoria's mom to have red hair since they are both dark-haired with a natural golden complexion. Victoria gets the shape of her face and sensual facial features from her mom and I am guessing her coloring comes from her dad. Rafe looks like he might have gotten his gray eyes from his mom's side.

The kitchen smells wonderful as Victoria and I sit down at the small table to dig into the homemade crisp. Monique asks me questions about Seattle and our move to New Orleans, about my mom, and if I have any other family.

"Rafe tells me that you are gifted like him." Monique drops the bomb very casually almost making me choke on my mouthful of food.

"Mom!" Victoria exclaims as she pats my back gently. "Are you ok?" She asks me. I nod at her and look at her mom in surprise as I allow myself to feel what she is feeling. She sincerely believes in Rafe's abilities and thinks that it is wonderful that he met me, another empath. Monique is a very compassionate woman who loves her family very much and is devoted to her charities so that she might help the less fortunate.

"I am," I reply with a warm smile. "Rafe is lucky to have a parent who knows and accepts his ability."

"Your father doesn't know?" She questions stunned that not all parents are as open-minded as she is. I shake my head with a sad smile.

"My mom warned me that he would never accept that part of me." I share with her.

"Your mom was an empath too?" Monique continues.

"Yes. She taught me a lot before she died." I explain. "I learned from a young age how to turn it off so that I am not bombarded all the time. I had never met someone like me before Rafe."

"He was very excited to tell us all about you yesterday." She shares with a knowing smile. I blush and focus on my dessert while both Monique and Victoria laugh.

"My parents know to keep it a secret from your dad," Victoria tells me.

"I wouldn't want to make you lie for me!" I exclaim uncomfortably.

"You and Rafe have a lot in common. I believe that you both can learn from each other." Monique smiles at me affectionately

Rafe grabs a small box off of the counter and sets it down in front of me with a smile.

"What's this?" I ask him curiously.

"It's your DNA kit." He tells me with a grin.

"We just talked about this yesterday!" I exclaim.

"I had an extra one. My uncle works for the lab so we can get the results quicker too." Rafe explains. "You can fill the vial in about a half hour or so." I am so envious of Rafe because he has a family that accepts him for the way he is. I have always wanted to tell my dad about my ability but trusted my mom to know best and kept it to myself.

Being around Monique makes me miss my mother because she is just as warm and loving as Mom was. Nicole's mom, my friend from Seattle, wasn't very maternal.

Victoria gives me a tour of the house that ends in her bedroom. She has a nice size room with a queen-size bed in dark blue with cream colored accents. She has a walk-in closet and a large mirrored dresser that has makeup and stuff scattered all over the top.

Her parents don't let her have a computer in her room or television, so her room is a little emptier than mine is. There is a bathroom in the hallway that she has to share with Rafe.

Feeling a little melancholy, I step over to one of her windows and look down onto the busy street to get control over my emotions. I haven't missed Mom this much in a long time. Monique reminds me of her. I can't keep from my mind the last two nights with my dad either. I was terrified that he wasn't going to stop when he did last night.

"Are you alright?" Victoria asks perceptively. I nod without turning around due to the tear that is trailing down my cheek.

"Your mom reminds me so much of mine." I manage to whisper as I feel choked up. "I haven't missed Mom this much in a long time."

"Well, she loves you so you can borrow her anytime you want to." She tells me as she rubs my back.

I laugh through my tears as I turn to look at her gratefully.

"You are a wonderful friend Victoria," I tell her sincerely.

"I know!" She jokes, faking superiority as she flips her hair dramatically.

THE CELESTIAL LOTUS

Dinner smells delicious as I follow Victoria into the dining room and see her dad there at the head of the table giving her mom a very seductive kiss.

"Dad!" Victoria exclaims with disgust. "You guys have a bedroom! Yuck!"

After finishing their kiss, he slaps Monique's butt playfully and gives Victoria an affectionate smile.

"You must be Journee." Her dad turns his warm smile on me. "You can call me Dimitri."

This is where Victoria and Rafe get their dark coloring from. Dimitri is very good-looking, just like his son and I am surprised to note that he has gray eyes as well. Rafe is merely a younger version of his dad.

"Antonescu is eastern European isn't it?" I ask him as I take a seat next to Victoria. Dimitri smiles at my interest.

"It is." He replies with just a hint of southern drawl to his deep voice. "My family comes from Romania, gypsies."

"My mother's maiden name was Dinescu." I share with a smile. "I believe that is Romanian as well."

"You don't have the golden complexion." Dimitri brings up. "Your father wasn't particularly pale."

"It's my eye color." I explain to him. "My mother had purple eyes with dark hair too and she also had porcelain skin. It's a condition called Alexandria's Genesis. I don't tan or burn in the sun at all."

"That's interesting." He nods as he gazes at me thoughtfully. "Your facial features are Romanian."

Rafe joins us at the table and sits on my other side while Monique brings the rest of the food to the table. She has made chicken Alfredo with broccoli but instead of pasta she has shaved zucchini into strips and steamed them. The combination is fantastic and a very healthy alternative.

I listen while their family chats with each other between bites of food and find myself missing the days when my mom was alive, and our family gathered every night for dinner. It is obvious that Victoria and Rafe come from a very loving home and they have welcomed me as if I am an adopted member.

Rafe and his dad talk about basketball while Victoria and her mom talk about the debutante club festivities that Monique has been organizing. Being the introvert that I am, I eat and listen happily while they all catch up with each other from a long week.

Victoria and I help her mom clean up after dinner before Rafe meets us in the living room to watch movies. The three of us curl up on the sectional, with me sitting between them of course, while Rafe starts the newest Avengers movie. Victoria groans at being forced to watch an action movie and I can see her disinterest considering she is a girly girl and doesn't have our psychic ability to draw her.

After the first movie is done, we all head into the kitchen to raid it for snacks to watch during the second movie. Rafe makes popcorn while Victoria grabs chips and dip and I carry the pop into the living room.

We settle into the second movie, a romantic comedy that Victoria has been dying to see. Not being a big popcorn fanatic, I share the chips and dip with Victoria, letting Rafe happily eat all of his popcorn by himself.

As soon as the romantic comedy is done Victoria gets up and makes a big show of yawning.

"I'm going to bed." She says. "I'm sure Rafe would like you to stay up and watch just one more movie." She states bluntly before she saunters from the room.

Suddenly shy, I drop my gaze to my lap and fiddle with the hem of my sweater while Rafe puts the next movie in, a horror flick. I hate horror movies and know I will be on his lap before long.

Tipping up my chin, Rafe gazes into my eyes intensely before he slowly lowers his head and kisses me softly. His lips move gently over mine and I tilt my head to the side before copying his movements. He wraps his arms around me tightly and touches his tongue to my bottom lip seeking entrance. I open to him and clutch the front of his shirt as he deepens the kiss passionately. We kiss for several moments and I can feel his heart racing under my palm as he responds to me. He finally lifts his head and kisses my forehead tenderly as he strokes my hair until he cools down. Disappointment rushes through me that I obviously didn't react to the kiss like he did.

"Wow." I whisper. "That was an amazing first kiss."

"I concur." He returns as he nuzzles my neck.

"We should probably watch the movie," I state logically as I feel myself becoming suddenly bashful wishing I felt as much passion as he did.

"You don't like scary movies." He says as he continues to kiss my neck and nibble on my earlobe.

"Cheater." I murmur, knowing he used his gift to gain that knowledge. He chuckles and reluctantly raises his head to smile down at me, his expression deeply sensual.

"I played it on purpose." He confesses as he strokes his thumb across my lower lip. "Come on. I will walk you up to the guest bedroom."

He turns off the television and I help him clean up all of our food and drinks before we head upstairs. At my door, he gives me a nearly chaste kiss on the lips before watching me enter my room.

"Watched movies with Victoria and Rafe. Going to bed now and wanted to let you know virtue is intact and I am safe." I text James as I lie in bed in my nightgown.

"Good girl." James texts me right back. *"Did you get your first kiss tonight?"*

"Yes. You were right about the fumbling." I confess to him.

"I'm sorry. Good night kiddo."

"Good night James."

I am jolted awake by Victoria plopping down on my bed.

"So?" She exclaims when I don't immediately respond to her.

"So what?" I grumble at her, so close to falling back asleep. Doesn't she sleep in like normal people?

"What happened after I went to bed last night?" She gushes impatiently.

"Please don't tell me you are one of those perky morning people!" I continue to grumble at her.

"Sorry." She apologizes, her voice bright and energetic. "Guilty as charged."

Reluctantly I sit up and stretch with an unhappy groan.

"We kissed on the couch almost as soon as you left the room," I confess to her without looking her in the face.

"And?" She enthuses. "I want details. Did you like it?"

I blush and shake my head, knowing since she is my best friend that I should share details.

"Yes. It was alright." I whisper as my blush deepens.

"Love at first sight." She sighs dramatically and flops onto her back with a goofy grin. "I finally get to have a sister."

"Whoa!" I exclaim, coming awake fully with her declaration. "We have been a couple for like twenty-four hours!"

"And you are made for each other!" She reasons with me. "You are both empaths and it was obvious you both felt something intense the first second you saw each other."

"Coffee," I tell her seriously. "If you want me conscious this early, I need coffee."

"Alright." She grins at me as I slip my robe on over my nightgown and follow her barefoot downstairs.

I am horrified to find Rafe already in the kitchen drinking a cup of coffee. I didn't even brush my hair! Pivoting on my heel I turn to rush back upstairs but Victoria grabs my hand and drags me back into the kitchen.

"You look adorably rumpled." She tells me as she pours me a cup of coffee and points to the cream and sugar before pointing at the chair next to Rafe. He looks up at me with that same seductive smile from last night and I blush a bright pink before sitting next to him.

I add cream and sugar to my coffee before taking a much-needed sip with a sigh of contentment. After a few moments of quiet, I turn to Rafe questioningly.

"You don't look like you want to be down here right now," I tell him, noting he looks as groggy as me.

"Nope." He agrees as he takes a sip of coffee. "She woke me up to drag me down here and make coffee."

"She must be a real joy on Christmas morning." I bring up, hiding my grin from Victoria.

"Hey!" She exclaims with her hands on her hips with a glare. Rafe and I both burst out laughing at her.

Monique walks into the kitchen and looks at Rafe with surprise.

"Victoria!" Monique scolds her daughter with a frown. "How many times have I told you to leave your brother alone?"

"How do you know I woke him up?" Victoria points out reasonably. "Maybe he is up early because he couldn't wait to see Journee?"

"You couldn't wait for him to see Journee," Monique states as she pours herself a cup of coffee.

"I think your mom knows you pretty well Victoria," I tell her with a saucy grin. "No getting out of that one."

"Please tell me she didn't wake you up too," Monique asks me as she raises her eyebrow at her daughter.

"Guilty." I nod as I take another sip of my coffee.

"You are the only teenager on this planet that doesn't want to sleep until noon," Monique tells Victoria as she ruffles her hair affectionately. "What did you guys want to do today besides visit Grams?"

Victoria and Rafe both shrug at the same time.

"It depends on what the newbie wants to do." Rafe says. "We don't know if she has seen any of the attractions or if she just wants to walk through the quarter and shop."

"If your grandmother's shop is already in the quarter we might as well walk around and check out the other shops," I suggest.

"Go get ready and meet down here in an hour," Monique says. "We can stop to eat somewhere."

Victoria squeals excitedly while I yawn widely and follow Rafe at a more sedate pace. Rafe takes a shower first and is out of the bathroom in just five minutes leaving it to me next. I manage to keep my shower down to ten minutes and slip into the guest room to finish getting ready so that Victoria can use the bathroom too.

"Good morning James." I text my bodyguard. *"We are going to the Celestial Lotus in the quarter and then going to look through the shops and probably stop somewhere to eat."*

"Good morning kiddo. I will be down there keeping an eye if you need me." James messages me back.

I French braid my wet hair and decide to just wear a pair of jeans, a t-shirt, and sneakers. After applying some light makeup, I throw on a jacket, put my cell in my coat pocket and my credit card in my jeans pocket.

Rafe is in the kitchen working on another cup of coffee when I walk in. He smiles at me and pulls me onto his lap.

"Good morning." He murmurs in his deep husky voice.

"Good morning." I giggle. "Are you awake now?"

He brushes his lips across mine softly. "Mmmmm." He murmurs before deepening the kiss passionately. I kiss him back and we don't hear the door to the kitchen open until we hear someone clear their throat. Looking up, I blush in horror at being caught by his dad. Rafe just laughs softly and strokes my back when I hide my face in the curve of his neck.

"Are you coming with us this morning?" Rafe asks his dad.

"I wish I could," Dimitri answers with a sigh. "I just got a lead on my case I have to check out."

"Be careful," Rafe tells him as his dad fills his coffee cup.

"Always son," Dimitri replies. "See you for dinner."

We end up waiting another twenty minutes for his mother and sister. Monique drives a black BMW sports car and Victoria insists that Rafe and I sit in the backseat together. I am surprised that she has no problems sharing my attention with her brother.

The Celestial Lotus is a small shop on a very busy street near Jackson Square, which is a really good location. I feel positive energy emanating from it as we approach the door.

The inside is bright and has a very wide-open feeling to it. I feel instantly welcomed and as if I am home somehow. Their grandmother hurries over and hugs everyone excitedly, even me. She looks to be in her fifties with silver hair she keeps in a long bob that falls just below her shoulders. Her eyes are a very piercing blue color and I know she sees things already that I am unsure if I want to hear.

She turns the open sign to closed and insists we join her for tea in the back room. After we have all exchanged pleasantries and sipped some of the aromatic tea, she turns to me with a serious expression on her face.

 Nadia begins with a fond smile. "James is a very important part of your life now and you must always trust him. You will be going through some trials and he will see you through all of them. You are like the daughter he never had. Allow him to discover your gift for himself. He will be very accepting and supportive, but make sure he figures it out for himself because he needs to come to terms about it in his mind."

"Wow." I breathe in awe. "You don't beat around the bush, do you?" I ask her, struggling to take in all she said.

"Tell me about your mom," Nadia says in a very soft voice. A tear trickles down my face at the tone of her voice. Something about it almost makes me think my mom is right here somehow.

"She was an empath too." I begin. "Monique is very much like she was. Mom just radiated beauty, compassion, innocence. She taught me how to control my gift as well as how to strengthen it. I miss her. We were inseparable."

"She is very proud of the woman you have become," Nadia tells me with an affectionate smile. "You will discover the secrets of your mother's past very soon, now tell me about Ansen."

"My dad and I have always been very close, until recently. He seems to be under a lot of stress lately and I don't think he is dealing with it very well." I blurt without thinking and then blush at my openness.

"You will learn more about what is going on with him soon," Nadia tells me as she gazes at me thoughtfully. When I try to read her and see what she is thinking about I hit a wall. My face must register my surprise because she shakes her head at me with a sad smile.

"There are things that I cannot tell you right now because you are not ready to hear them." She explains to me gently.

"I'm sorry," I tell her as I feel as if I were being rude.

"No need to apologize my dear," Nadia reassures me. "You merely wanted to know what I was thinking about. Some events must take place before I can tell you more."

"Will I be alright?" I ask her bluntly. Nadia smiles at me affectionately.

"Yes Journee." She takes my hand in hers and squeezes tenderly. "Some of these events will cause you great pain, but you will come out the other side a wiser and stronger woman for it."

MORE THAN AN EMPATH

I take some time to wander around the shop while Nadia talks with Rafe privately. Rafe doesn't look very happy with whatever she is saying though. Learning that James will be an important part of my life makes me very happy because I like him; he is like a father figure to me. I have a bad feeling about what was missing, however. Nadia never once said that my father would help me through any of these trials. Is he going to die too?

My stomach clenches as I contemplate what kind of pain, she is talking about that I will be going through. Instantly, a memory of Dad's nightly visits to my room pops in my head, but I brush it away. He would never hurt me. Besides, why would dad hire a bodyguard for me and have him sleep in the house if I were in danger from him?

Rafe steps up behind me and wraps his arms around me, holding me tenderly.

"We name our first daughter after Grams," Rafe whispers into my ear. I turn around in his arms and gaze up at him in awe.

"Seriously?" I ask him, emotion choking me up slightly. He nods and strokes my cheek gently. Having him give me a small taste of the future helps me to face whatever trials may be down the road. That and the fact that James will be there to help me as well.

"You are not just an empath Journee," Nadia states as she comes into the shop quietly.

"What do you mean?" I ask her curiously.

"Your mother was only an empath and she taught you how to use those gifts, but an empath cannot hear actual thoughts from the person she is reading as you can," Nadia explains to me. "You don't allow yourself to listen in on what someone is thinking because you think it is an invasion of their privacy. You are a very powerful psychic my dear."

"Are you sure?" I ask her, not sure if I should believe her.

"Tell me about Heath," Nadia says with a grim smile.

I glance at Rafe uncomfortably because what I will say will anger him.

"Rafe is not angry at you Journee because you did nothing wrong." Nadia encourages me. "Tell me about Heath."

"He came up behind me and Victoria when we were standing in line for lunch. He said hi to me and when I turned to look at him the arrogance on his face made me read him, just for protective purposes." I pause and look down at the floor, not wanting to say more.

"What did you hear and see Journee?" Nadia presses me gently.

"He thought *'I want to tap that. I bet she is still a cherry.'* He visualized raping me while I struggled to get away from him." I confess, still staring at the floor.

Instantly I can feel the rage coming off of Rafe in waves.

"Rafe!" Nadia scolds him. "Control your emotions!"

Rafe's emotional overload is suddenly gone and I can't read anything from him as he puts up a protective wall against me. He embraces me tighter and kisses the top of my head.

"I'm sorry." He whispers. "I am not upset with you Journee."

"Are you sure?" I ask him anxiously.

"You are innocent, babe," Rafe reassures me.

"What sort of readings do you get from Ansen?" Nadia asks me, her voice strangely different.

"You know I can't read him," I state nervously. "Do you know why?"

"When a psychic or an empath is unable to read someone, it is because there is a brain defect, injury, or the person has some sort of mental disorder that doesn't allow it," Nadia explains. "It isn't because of his relationship with you."

"He has never stated that anything was wrong with him." I share honestly.

"Your psychic gift needs some development Journee," Nadia tells me seriously. "It is not an invasion of someone's privacy in all cases. If you don't wish to check and see what Victoria is thinking I can understand that. Develop your gift on people you go to school with or someone you see in the store or walking down the street. A good example is what you did when you went out to eat with Ansen your first night here in New Orleans. That poor woman you focused on during dinner. That is a good way to strengthen that ability."

"I wanted to help her," I confess sadly as I remember how terrified she was.

"You were also too frightened to listen to the man's thoughts, weren't you?" Nadia asks.

"Her fear was enough. Knowing what caused her fear was nearly too much for me to handle. I really didn't want to know what he was thinking." I share with her.

"Did Uncle Ben come and pick up her DNA kit last night?" Nadia asks Rafe.

"Yep." Rafe nods at her.

"Good." Nadia seems very pleased with this bit of information.

"You have seen my results already," I state as I gaze at her curiously. "Good or bad?" I ask her hesitantly.

"A bit of both actually," Nadia tells me honestly. "But that is all I will say for the moment. I will tell you that your instinct to not share this information with Ansen is correct, however."

I nod, grateful that she confirmed my suspicion that Dad won't understand.

Nadia steps up to me and pulls me out of Rafe's arms and into hers, embracing me affectionately. Pulling back slightly, she looks down into my eyes with love shining in hers.

"You are already accepted as a part of our family Journee." She says with a catch in her voice. "Please come to me with anything that you may need. I have already been waiting a long time to meet you, my dear."

"How long have you known about me?" I ask her, brushing a happy tear from my cheek.

"Before my children were born." She confesses to me with an emotional smile.

"I wasn't even born yet." I gasp, awestruck.

"No." Nadia chuckles softly. "Your life was destined to be intertwined with mine. Now then, enough seriousness for one day. Go! Shop and have some fun today like teenagers are supposed to do."

"You said my mother is proud of me." I turn back to Nadia at the door.

"She is," Nadia confirms with a mysterious smile. "But that is a conversation to be had in the future, not today."

Walking back up to Nadia I hug her emotionally and kiss her cheek as yet another tear trickles down my face.

"Thank you, Nadia," I exclaim, affection obvious in my voice.

"Oh, it's Grams to you girl!" Nadia wipes away her own tear as she shoves me out the door with everyone else.

Out of the corner of my eye, I see Monique try to wipe away a tear of her own nonchalantly. We walk from shop to shop through the quarter where I mainly just window shop at all of the cool things for sale here. I buy a lavender sundress that I just can't live without, a cell phone case for my iPhone, and a beautiful opal necklace that just seems to call to me.

We stop for lunch at a local diner that specializes in poor boy sandwiches. Considering that we all skipped breakfast everyone practically inhales their food in record timing. We sit and enjoy the sunshine on the outdoor patio while Monique talks about the history of New Orleans and how it became famous for being a paranormal hotspot.

Since we are so close to Jackson Square everyone insists, we should walk through the cathedral as it is a must-see here in New Orleans. I have to admit that it is absolutely breathtaking. I step away from everyone and step closer to the altar so I can light a candle for my mom. Whenever Dad and I went to church I would always light a candle in her memory.

I have just finished my brief prayer and am rising from my knees when I see someone lighting a candle next to me. He is a giant of a man with a shaved head and a full dark brown beard. As I get a closer look something about him tickles my memory, but I shrug it off and turn to leave.

"Excuse me, lass, ye dropped this." He states politely in a thick Irish accent as he holds out my credit card.

"Oh!" I wonder how that fell out of my jeans pocket. "Thank you!"

I smile at him and nod my thanks before hurrying away.

My mind is whirling with everything that Grams told me this morning while we walk around the French quarter. I am trying to make sense of things as well as wondering about the things she wouldn't share with me yet. I cannot get over the fact that she never mentioned my father helping me through any of my trials. Why is it only James I am supposed to trust?

Rafe, since he can access my emotions, knows I am a bit overwhelmed processing everything, so he stays close to me, but allows me my mental privacy. Victoria absolutely loves shopping, no big surprise there, so she has been in heaven all day. Monique seems to know all the shop owners, so she has chatted with each of them.

We wander back to the car and to my surprise, our next stop for the day is the Audubon Zoo. Being that I am an empath I love animals for their peaceful natures as well as the fact that I am not overloaded being around them. Rafe's face registers his joy too and I can guess he loves the animals for the same reason.

Since this is my first visit to this zoo everyone lets me set the pace and spend as much time on each exhibit as I wish to. The orangutans are hilarious to watch with each other. The white alligators are really cool, I had no idea they even existed. I love the leopards and the tigers, although I can feel their unhappiness at being caged. Kneeling right next to the glass the tiger walks up to me and we stare into each other's eyes for several minutes while everyone else just watches in amazement. Without realizing what I am doing I endeavor to send the big cat a measure of comfort and that I understand how it feels. It raises its large plate-sized paw to the glass between us and I feel his acceptance of me. I place my hand on the glass right on his paw as a tear trickles down my face.

"You are communicating with it," Rafe states in amazement. "How are you doing that?" He says so only I can hear him.

"I don't know." I shrug. "I have always been able to. He wants to be free."

We move on to the rest of the exhibits, but the tiger stays in my thoughts.

I have always wanted a pet, but Dad has always been against it for numerous reasons. I can't wait until I live on my own because that is the first thing I am going to do.

As soon as we get back to the Antonescu house I retreat to the guest room because I have an overwhelming need to be alone. They all respect my privacy even though I know Rafe is having a hard time allowing me my alone time because he wants to help me feel better.

"You looked upset today. Are you alright?" James texts me as soon as I flop on the bed. I smile knowing he was keeping a close eye on me.

"Victoria's mom reminds me of mine. I have been very melancholy today." I text back to him, knowing I cannot tell him anything else, but at least I can be honest about that.

"I'm sorry kiddo." James messages back sincerely.

"Did you enjoy the zoo? Lol." I tease him, knowing he was probably there somewhere.

"Brat. Yes, actually I did. The tiger was very educational." James states, leaving me to wonder what he thought of my interaction with the big cat.

"I don't think he liked his cage very much," I reply, not admitting to anything.

"Are you staying in for the night?"

"Yes. I think we are going to mass tomorrow morning."

"Ok. Behave yourself tonight." James texts back including a winking emoticon. I stick my tongue out at my phone but don't text him back.

After a couple hours Victoria knocks on the door before poking her head in.

"Can I come in?" She asks hesitantly. I nod and she grins excitedly before running across the room to plop down on the bed next to me.

"Are you going to be alright?" She asks seriously.

"Yeah." I sigh. "It upsets me that your grams never said that my dad will help me through my trials. Only that James is the one to trust. Is my dad going to die too?"

"No, not my grams." Victoria corrects me. "She's your grams too."

I smile at her affectionately.

"Why didn't you tell me about Heath?" Victoria asks curiously.

"It freaked me out," I exclaim. "I guess I just wanted to forget I even heard it. The visual made me want to puke. I hate to imagine what any of the girls went through that he raped because that is what he likes. He likes to force himself on a girl, it's what gets him off."

"Come on down to dinner." Victoria smiles at me. "Mom made fried chicken."

As soon as I walk into the dining room, I feel Rafe in my mind making sure I am alright.

"I'm fine Rafe." I sit down next to him and kiss him on the cheek.

"I'm sorry." He says guiltily.

"You don't have to apologize. You're just worried about me after everything Grams said." I reassure him. "It's a lot for me to take in."

"I met James today." Rafe's father Dimitri tells me after avidly watching our exchange.

"Oh," I state, wondering why he shared that with me. "Why?"

"Your father wants to be sure you are safe while you are here so he gave me James' number so we could talk," Dimitri explains.

"Do you know why I suddenly needed a bodyguard after moving here to New Orleans when I didn't need one in Seattle?" I ask him bluntly.

"I do." Rafe's father replies in a gravely serious tone that gives me goosebumps. I grab Rafe's hand for support as a strange feeling of impending doom comes over me.

"Will you tell me?" I whisper hesitantly, not really sure if I want to know but know for certain Dimitri wants to share this.

"Your father somehow angered the Irish mob up there in Seattle," Dimitri explains. "They threatened him, which is why he moved you both down here so suddenly. James is an ex-navy seal and has protected some pretty important people."

"Why isn't James protecting Dad?" I suggest logically.

"A member of the mob was seen following you in Seattle," Dimitri tells me seriously. My face pales. Is this one of the trials that Grams was talking about? Is this why I am supposed to trust James?

"Was Dad agreeable to my spending the weekend because you are an FBI agent?" I ask him honestly. Dimitri nods his head.

"I have invited James to work with me on the mob because I have federal clearance that he doesn't have," Dimitri explains to me. "Their organization is called The Incorporated. The leader's name was Connor O'Shea, but he was killed in a federal raid two weeks ago. It is believed that your father is responsible for the tip that led to that raid. Connor's younger brother Quinn has taken over as leader and rumor has it that he is after you for revenge."

"Why me?" I ask in confusion. "I didn't do anything to these people. I am not responsible for the death of this man's brother."

"No, you are not, but your father is very close to you just like the O'Shea brothers were," Dimitri says.

"Why didn't James explain all of this to me?" I want to know.

"He and I discussed that today. I pointed out to him that it would benefit us if you were aware of the potential danger you are in." He replies. "I am aware of your gifts even if James is not at this point. I believe that helps to keep you safe."

Dimitri opens a file folder on the table in front of him and hands me a stack of photographs. They are large 8 x 10's of men. I look up at him questioningly.

"The top photo is of Quinn O'Shea, the new leader of the Incorporated. The rest of them are top-ranking members and could be the ones he will use to attempt to grab you." He says with a sigh.

I look down at the top picture and feel my heart race with fear. This is the man who wants revenge on my dad. He has auburn hair that is buzzed on the sides and is long enough on top to see it is wavy. He has an oval face with a wide forehead and a hooded brow over dark eyes. His nose is straight over full lips with a strong jaw covered in a well-groomed beard. His shoulders look wide and he just looks like he is a very large man, muscle-wise. I expected him to look like an old man, but he looks like he is only in his mid-twenties at the oldest.

I flip through the rest of the pictures and try to commit them to memory but there are just too many of them. Looking up I see that everyone at the table is gazing at me worriedly.

"You are going to tell me that Quinn is here in New Orleans, aren't you?" I ask Dimitri, my voice trembling with fear.

"I cannot say that for a certainty." He answers me honestly. "My sources in Seattle tell me that he has disappeared. Only a skeleton crew remain in Seattle to conduct his business there. Starting on Monday James will protect you personally while two FBI agents will be assigned to you twenty-four hours a day. James will be inside the school and follow you from class to class while two agents will be outside the school at all times. When you are at home there will be two agents on your property as well."

"Is this necessary?" I ask incredulously.

"Do you know what the O'Shea's do to make the most money?" Dimitri asks, struggling to keep the anger from his voice. I shake my head, terrified of the answer.

"The Incorporated run strip clubs and prostitution rings. Most of the girls are bought off of the black market after they have been abducted from their families and loved ones; never to be seen again." Dimitri tells me, his helpless fury lacing his voice.

SHARING SECRETS

After dinner, Victoria insists on helping her mom clean up the kitchen while Rafe takes me into the living room where we curl up on the couch together. He tells me all about his childhood, his thoughts and dreams, school, and his relationships with his family. I reciprocate and share all of the same things with him. I get a bit emotional when I talk about my mom and how my dad and I have drifted apart in the last few weeks. I tell him all about school in Seattle, my friend Nicole, my thoughts and dreams, and my wishes for the future.

Changing the subject, I explain to him in detail my strange reaction to the picture of Quinn O'Shea. The strange fear I felt made me think something bad is going to happen with this man. My fear is that my dad will die during all of this and I will be an orphan with no family.

Rafe holds me while I sob uncontrollably after holding in my emotions all day long, beginning with my talk with Grams. I am hiccupping by the time my tears finally dry up and I have completely soaked the front of Rafe's shirt.

I wake the next morning in the guest room still wearing the clothes from the day before and Rafe is sleeping on the floor next to the bed. I look around in confusion because I don't remember falling asleep. Rafe rolls over and opens his eyes with a yawn then smiles at me in that sexy way of his. Blushing, I push my hair away from my face and look away from him bashfully.

"Thank you for sleeping in here," I tell him and then gasp when he plops on the bed with me.

"You're very welcome." He hugs me and nuzzles my neck. "Victoria is going to burst in here at any second to tell us to get ready for mass."

I hug him back and just lie my head on his shoulder with a contented sigh. Sure enough, not even five minutes later Victoria knocks on the door before she pokes her head in with a grin. She hops into the room with a squeal when she sees we are both awake.

"I don't remember falling asleep last night," I murmur, not moving my head from Rafe's shoulder.

"Dad had mom spike your juice with a sleeping pill," Victoria says. "Rafe was worried that you wouldn't be able to sleep with everything you were feeling."

"She gave me a sleeping pill?" I ask, surprised.

"It was one of those melatonin things," Victoria explains. "It's something that your body already produces and is perfectly safe with no reactions."

"I'm going to go take a quick shower," Rafe says as he strokes my back. "Will you be alright?"

I nod as I sit back and watch him leave the room. Victoria looks at me seriously.

"Are you alright, really?" She wants to know. "You really got dumped on yesterday between my dad and Grams."

"Yeah. I mean there really isn't anything I can do about the stuff that Grams told me. If she thought I were truly in danger she probably would have said something." I explain. "The stuff your dad told me was important and my knowledge about it will help me to stay on the alert and not do something stupid."

"I don't know how you stay so calm." She states as she shakes her head skeptically. "I would be in a total panic."

"Did you see me crying on your brother last night?" I bring it up in a sarcastic tone. Victoria chuckles.

"I did." She looks sad. "I felt so bad."

"Well, I feel a lot better now that I let it out, I can tell you that!" I exclaim. "Should I wear my new lavender dress to mass?" I ask her as I get out of bed and hold it up. She nods her head eagerly.

"It's perfect!" She says as she looks at it thoughtfully. "I have a white cardigan that will go with it, make it look a little more Catholic."

"Catholic?" I ask with a laugh. "What does that mean?"

"You know......like a nun......Catholic." Victoria tips her head to the side thoughtfully.

My phone vibrates and I pick it up off the bedside table and see that James has messaged me.

"You didn't tell me good night last night kiddo."

"Sorry. I got so upset they felt the need to give me melatonin after dinner." I share with him honestly.

"Wow!" Victoria exclaims as she reads my phone over my shoulder. "He's awesome! You got really close with him, already didn't you?"

"I really did," I confess to her. "We connected right away and it's almost like we have known each other our whole lives or something. It's weird."

"Your father wanted to keep this a secret from you but both Dimitri and I thought it wise to fill you in. Are you alright, really?" James messages back.

I'm afraid, really afraid, but you have a way of making me feel safe. I know you would do anything for me." I share with my bodyguard sincerely. *"Are you coming to mass?"*

"Yes, kiddo, although you won't see me."

I smile as I put the phone down and Rafe walks back into the room wearing only a pair of pajama bottoms. He is so good looking I just want to drool. His dark hair is still damp and looks like he ran his fingers through it to keep it back off of his face. He is over a foot taller than me and without his shirt, I can see that he spends a lot of time lifting weights. His chest, shoulders, and abs are wonderfully defined making me want to run my fingers over them.

"Do you want me to leave you two alone?" Victoria teases me, jarring me out of my reverie. "Yuck!"

I blush while Rafe laughs loudly as he steps up to me and kisses me on the forehead.

"Go take a shower babe." He tells me as he shoves Victoria playfully.

Rafe leaves the room, followed by Victoria as I hurry into the shower, so I don't make everyone late. I am out of the shower, dressed, my hair braided, and ready to leave in just twenty minutes. Victoria is known to be slow, so I make my way down to the kitchen where Rafe and his parents are already drinking coffee and eating beignets.

I grab one of the pastries off of the counter with an eager smile because I have yet to try one. New Orleans is known for them and after my first bite, I can see why. I moan with pleasure as Rafe wipes some powdered sugar off of my lips.

"Good?" He asks, his eyes sparkling happily. I nod and moan again blissfully, careful to keep the powdered sugar off of my clothes.

"We need to take you to the Café du Monde," Monique tells me with a warm smile. "They are even better there."

"Did you make these?" I ask curiously. I had just assumed she bought them from somewhere.

"I did." She replies.

"I couldn't imagine them any yummier," I tell her honestly.

"You might want to go rush your daughter," Dimitri tells Monique as he gazes at his watch pointedly.

"My daughter," Monique states with false irritation. "Why is it every time she is running late, she is my daughter?" She walks to the door and Dimitri swats her on the butt causing her to yelp in surprise.

"Because you were always late until you had my help," Dimitri states firmly.

Victoria rushes into the kitchen and grabs a beignet off of the plate and hurries out of the kitchen while we all follow along behind her.

I am actually surprised that we are going to mass at St Louis Cathedral in Jackson Square, although with Monique's love for New Orleans history it shouldn't have. There are so many people in attendance that I wouldn't have been able to see James even if I wanted to.

We are early enough that I get to go and light a candle for my mother like I always did in Seattle. Rafe and Dimitri flank me and watch the crowds while I kneel there and say a small prayer for my mom.

It's nice to just allow myself to follow along as the priest talks and not have to worry about my troubles for a short time.

After mass, Rafe and Dimitri stay close to me while Monique and Victoria walk around and chat with people. I use the time to practice my psychic ability like Grams suggested I do while I am in public.

I notice a middle-aged man who is standing off by himself that seems out of place somehow. He is looking around at everyone, sort of like I am so I decide to take a peek inside his head to see what he is thinking about.

"The boss is going to pay me big for finding the Parisi girl."

I can feel all the color drain from my face as unconsciously I grab Rafe by the hand and share the man's thought with Rafe mentally so he can hear it too. Knowing that I cannot react visibly to the man finding me I stand perfectly still while Rafe tells his father softly and Dimitri calls James.

Nonchalantly, Rafe and Dimitri manage to get Monique and Victoria's attention, so they join us while we wait for permission to leave the church. James appears out of nowhere flanked by six FBI agents who escort the five of us out to a black SUV parked at the curb.

I have no idea what happens to the man I identified but the Antonescu's are dropped off at home while I am taken immediately back to my house. No big surprise when I see that Dad is not home once again. James takes me up to my room and sits me down on the bed while he paces in front of me in agitation. Finally, he turns to look at me with a look of complete disbelief on his face.

"I was watching you standing there with Rafe and Dimitri," James says, his voice confused. "I watched you look around and notice the guy standing off by himself then grab Rafe by the hand. You didn't say a word and Rafe didn't notice the guy until you grabbed his hand. Rafe spoke quietly to his dad and then Dimitri called me to tell me that man was watching you for his boss."

My face pales and I look away from him uncomfortably as he kneels down in front of me.

"How did Rafe know that he was one of the mob's men Journee?" James asks. "You are the one who found him, but you didn't say a word to Rafe, but every muscle in your body was screaming for you to run."

I shake my head as tears begin to flow unchecked down my cheeks. James takes my hands in his tenderly and strokes the back of my hands with his thumbs.

"Your first day of school when I asked if you needed help with homework you *told* me I was good at math after you looked at me strangely. The next morning you *said* I was impressed with Rafe before I got a chance to share that with you; again, after you looked at me strangely. That afternoon when I wanted to talk to you about not rushing into things with Rafe you repeated word for word what I had just thought; again after you gave me one of your strange looks."

I shake my head at him again, too terrified to say anything.

"Being a navy seal, I was trained to notice details that no one else would notice because it could mean the difference between life and death." James continues to speak to me gently. "I noticed your little slips right away, but I have to admit that I didn't want to believe what it really meant. Each time it happened again I had to face the facts and really keep an open mind, but this morning in church really convinced me because I saw it with my own eyes."

I peek at him hesitantly and see him gazing at me with his heart in his eyes, pleading with me to trust him. Grams told me to trust him.

"What was the man thinking Journee?" James asks me bluntly.

"The boss is going to pay me big for finding the Parisi girl." I recite as I hope he doesn't look at me like I am a freak. Instead of reacting the way I expect, James pulls me down onto his lap and holds me while I cry.

"It's OK little one," James whispers into my hair as he holds me tightly. "I believe you."

I listen in to his thoughts just to be sure and I am amazed that he truly believes in my gift.

"Dad doesn't know, and you can't tell him because he won't understand," I whisper to James once my tears have dried up.

"My lips are sealed kiddo." He vows as he looks down at me with new eyes.

DAD

Monday morning finds me terrified to go to school and James has to finally come up to my bedroom to get me.

"I want to stay home," I tell him as I sit on my bed in my school uniform, my bag next to me. "Where is my dad? I waited up for him, did he even come home last night?"

"You have to continue on with your life kiddo."

"Why isn't my dad working with you and Dimitri? Aren't I more important than his stupid law practice? I'm afraid." I confess as I look up at my huge bodyguard. His rugged appearance would have frightened me just a week ago but now I feel protected.

"I know you are, and I will be outside each classroom today and even looking over your shoulder at lunch watching Rafe wish he could kiss you." James teases me, not answering any of my questions about my father.

"James!" I exclaim in horror.

"Come on Journee." He encourages me seriously now. I sigh and slide off of the bed and take the hand he offers to me. I hold his hand tightly feeling like a little kid again.

James stops in the foyer and takes out a two-way radio while he holds me close to his side.

"We are ready." He states into the radio.

Someone replies. "All clear."

James opens the door and walks me down the steps and to my shock I see FBI agents all over the place. Parked at the curb is a black SUV instead of the limousine James normally drives me to school in.

"Where is the limo?" I ask curiously as I try to keep pace as we practically jog to the vehicle.

"For the foreseeable future, we will be working with the FBI to keep you safe," James explains. "We still don't know where Quinn O'Shea is."

He helps me into the back seat and slides in next to me while an agent slides in on the other side of me.

"I will be outside each of your classes today while there will be agents outside the window of each one. There will also be agents on the roof and walking the school grounds. Until further notice, the school is on complete lockdown. All of the doors will be locked once school starts with two agents assigned to each door. No one is allowed in or out unless verified." James explains to me on the ride to school.

When we walk up to the school, I see two agents using a metal detector wand on each person before they are allowed to enter the school. Just inside the door, two more agents are searching each and every bag before they are cleared. There is a tote next to them where they are putting items that are not allowed to be brought into the building.

I feel bad that everyone has to go through this because of me.

"You should have just let me stay home for a while," I tell James as he walks me to the front of the line. "I can do my schoolwork at home until all of this blows over."

"The FBI is hoping this will draw him out and enable them to catch him," James explains.

"Great," I exclaim sarcastically as my bag is searched. "I am being used as bait."

I stalk upstairs to my locker where Victoria and Rafe are waiting for me.

"Are you alright?" Rafe asks as he pulls me into his arms. I curl contentedly against him and lie my face on his chest with a sigh.

"I am now," I murmur as he squeezes me tightly.

He lets me go and I reluctantly open my locker, place all of my books in it from my bag, grab what I need for the first hour, and shut the door. Rafe hurries away to his first-class and Victoria and I head down the hallway towards ours. James stays a few paces behind us, no doubt on high alert even though there shouldn't be any threats inside the school.

Heath steps up to me and I see James start to approach so I hold up my hand for him to wait.

"You are going to get yours for humiliating me." He threatens me arrogantly.

"I'm not the one who is going to getting what I deserve." I step closer to him so I can lower my voice.

"I know about the girls you have raped," I whisper. "Your rich family can't buy you out of this one. They like pretty boys like you in the pen."

I give him a shove and when he moves to do something in retaliation, I let him get close enough for me to knee him in the groin. I hear all of his breath leave in a whoosh as he doubles over in agony.

"Don't *ever* presume to think you can lay hands on me," I state in a calm voice as I step away from him.

To my surprise, a crowd has gathered to witness Heath's further humiliation at my hands and all of the girl's present applaud me. I keep my face lowered because I don't want people thinking I enjoyed what I did. Violence has its place. The clapping is joined by many cheering as finally Heath the Creep is getting his just dues.

I sit down at my desk in English class as my phone vibrates.

"Well done kiddo." James messages me.

"I wish he hadn't forced me to do that." I text back.

"That is why I am proud of you." He replies.

Being that I am such an introvert I really hate it when I am the center of attention. With the situation with Heath, all of the girls and a lot of the guys here treat me like I am some sort of savior. To my surprise, everyone at school has already heard about the near mob abduction at church yesterday and everyone is gossiping about it. I am looked at as if I am some sort of royalty because of my personal bodyguard and all of the FBI agents here to protect me.

I keep myself focused in my classes, so my mind is off of everything else and the rest of the morning passes without incident. James is always outside my classroom waiting for me as is Rafe. All of the other students adapt pretty quickly to the lockdown and by the time lunch rolls around the FBI agents are ignored.

I really don't want to eat, but unfortunately, James and Rafe are a step ahead of me and insist I at least eat a salad or something. I manage a few bites, but my stomach rebels, and I rush to the bathroom only to see that it is out of order. James is following behind me as I run down the hallway and around the corner by the band room, where the next closest bathroom is located.

I slip into the bathroom and barely manage to vomit in one of the toilets.

"Are you alright kiddo?" James opens the door just enough to yell in.

"Better," I call out to him. "Give me a few minutes to make sure I don't need to get sick again."

"I'm out here if you need me." He closes the door with a click.

I rinse my mouth out a couple times in the sink and splash my face to cool myself off. Feeling good enough to go back to the lunchroom I turn towards the door leading into the hallway and run into a very large person. Before I can utter a peep, I am pushed up against the wall and a knife is pressed up to my throat.

"It's quiet ye'll be lass." A deep husky voice in a thick Irish brogue whispers into my ear. He is pressed up against me and I swear I can feel each and every muscle definition in his chest. I look up, my heart racing in terror, and recognize Quinn O'Shea from the photograph Dimitri showed me.

"Quinn!" I gasp in a tiny whisper as I instinctively grab the arm that is holding the knife to my throat.

"Och, I'm pleased to see no introduction is necessary." He whispers as he gazes down at me heatedly, his accent so thick I have a hard time understanding him.

He looks even younger in person than he did in the picture. He only looks a few years older than me and he also looks much larger as he towers over my tiny frame. I have never thought guys with red hair were attractive, but Quinn is a completely different story, which makes me ponder my own sanity.

Peeking into his thoughts I hear his amazement at how lovely I am and that he may have to change his plans for me. I gasp at the amount of rage and hatred he feels for my father. Quinn wants to hurt my father and knows he can do it through me. I expected to feel more negative qualities to the head of a crime mob, but I am confused by the compassion he feels towards me.

"Are you going to kill me?" I whimper as I arch my neck away from the blade.

"Oh no." He smiles down at me his brown eyes intensely seductive. "I have other plans for us lassie. I wanted to come and introduce myself."

I blush at the intimate thoughts that are flicking through his mind and avert my gaze over his shoulder.

"Bashful." He murmurs in approval as he leans closer and nuzzles my cheek softly.

"Are you doing alright kiddo?" James' voice calls inside the room.

Quinn places his hand on my mouth as he gazes into my eyes threateningly as he pushes the knife against my skin just a bit harder.

"Doona make me hurt ye, Journee." Quinn stares down at me pleadingly. I can feel his regret at the thought of having to harm me as he really wants to save me instead of allowing Ansen to have me, whatever that means. His feeling of disgust for my father rushes over me making me cringe.

"Yep," I reply when Quinn removes his hand from my mouth. "I'm just splashing my face to cool down, so my nausea goes away."

I hear the door close and feel Quinn physically relax as he smiles down at me with approval. He removes the knife from my throat and places it in a sheath at his waist, pins my wrists above my head before I can struggle, and leans into me, nearly crushing me into the wall behind me as he slams his mouth down on mine. He squeezes my wrists together painfully when I refuse to open to his tongue and with a frightened moan, I allow him access. He quickly deepens the kiss and plunders the inside of my mouth while I desperately try to keep my tongue in the back of my throat. He tastes like whiskey as he tries to draw a response from me. I am trembling so much that if he didn't have me pinned to the wall I would no doubt fall to the floor.

One second, he is nearly bruising my lips under his with his tongue deep in my mouth and the next he is just gone.

"James!" I scream as I sink to the floor and dissolve into tears. He is there almost instantly and is kneeling in front of me. I point to the door leading into the band room and desperately try to catch my breath to speak again.

"Quinn." I manage to croak. "Go."

James yells into his two-way radio and waits a couple seconds until several FBI agents enter from the hallway before he follows Quinn into the band room. One FBI agent stays with me while the others follow James.

After a few minutes, Rafe and Victoria rush into the bathroom and Rafe picks me up in his arms to carry me out of the bathroom. I cannot stop crying as he carries me out to a waiting SUV. Victoria has stayed behind to grab my stuff from my locker and to gather the homework I will need for the foreseeable future.

Instead of going home, I am brought to the Antonescu house where Dimitri is waiting for me with a bunch of agents in place for my protection. "My presence here puts all of you in danger." I protest when I finally stop crying.

"He won't hurt anyone to get to you if he can help it," Dimitri explains to me after Rafe sits down on the sofa with me cradled on his lap. "He has a very different code of honor than his brother Connor did."

"He thought something strange," I tell Dimitri. "I asked him if he was going to kill me and he thought that he wanted to save me so Ansen couldn't have me himself. He meant that my dad wanted me as more than a daughter."

Confused and upset I curl up in Rafe's lap not wanting to ever leave the house again. Dad hasn't been here for me at all during this whole thing. Something hard is poking into my thigh and I reach into my blazer pocket and find a USB drive in there.

"This isn't mine," I state, my stomach clenching again as I wonder what is on this. "Quinn must have put this in my pocket." I hand it over to Dimitri and he hurries into his office with it while I stay on the sofa with Rafe, too afraid to see what is on it.

After a half-hour, Dimitri steps back into the living room and gives me a very emotional look.

"You need to see this Journee, I'm sorry." He motions for me to follow him.

James is waiting for me in Dimitri's office and scoops me up in his arms as soon as I step into the room.

"I'm so sorry." He whispers into my ear. "I should have checked the bathroom first, but you had to get sick so badly I let you have your privacy."

"It's not your fault James," I reassure him as I cling to him.

Dimitri has a video paused on the large screen television that is attached to the far wall and when James sits down with me cradled on his lap, he resumes it. I watch as my dad appears on the screen talking to a very large man with red hair that I am guessing must be Quinn's brother Connor.

Dad is talking to Connor about Mom and how she deceived him when they first met. He is furious that I am not really his daughter. He talks about how he is going to get his revenge on Sasha by poisoning her to get her out of the way. He then goes on to arrogantly brag about how he is going punish my mother by brutally taking my virginity from me when I grow up. Images of Dad coming into my room our first two nights in New Orleans flood my mind and makes me feel sick again.

"Oh god!" I moan. "I should have told you."

"Tell me what Journee?" James asks, his tone strangely aggressive.

"Our first couple nights in New Orleans, Dad....I mean, Ansen came into my room while I was asleep." I explain, shame filling me. "He crawled into bed with me like he was sleepwalking and looking for Mom. He kept calling out her name."

"What did he do to you?" James asks while everyone else in the room is waiting anxiously to hear my answer.

"He was lying almost completely on top of me until I could barely breathe. There was no way I could yell. He stroked my hair and pinned me to the bed. I felt so bad for him because I thought he truly missed Mom."

"I am sure he was counting on you feeling that way," Dimitri states gently. "I have just met you and I know the depths of your compassion for people."

"Where is he? Where is Ansen?" I murmur in a tiny voice.

"We suspect that Quinn's men have him," Dimitri says. "No one has seen him since Saturday."

I squirm off of James' lap and walk towards the door when James grabs me from behind.

"Where are you going kiddo?" He demands, his voice gruff.

"I need to be alone," I whisper my reply, not wanting to break down and cry in front of all these people. James lets me go but gestures to Rafe and signals to one of the FBI agents to follow.

I go upstairs to the guest bedroom but before I can step into the room I notice James has followed us and he goes in and sweeps it to be extra sure of my safety. He hands me an extra two-way radio and sternly lectures Rafe to not leave me alone under any circumstances.

I can feel James' self-recrimination because Quinn got his hands on me today and he is so furious he is having trouble controlling his need for violence. My need to comfort him makes me step up to him before he closes the door behind him.

"Hey!" I state with an extra ounce of sass in my voice. James turns to look at me and his expression doesn't soften like it normally does.

I step up to him and lift my hand to his cheek and rub my thumb across his whiskers tenderly.

"I'm fine." I lecture him. "So, stop it!"

"Journee!" He says, his voice breaking. "He could have killed you."

"He doesn't want to kill me he wants to save me," I inform him gently. "Quinn thinks he is saving me from Ansen."

"Are you certain?" He questions me.

"Yes. In the bathroom today I was confused because he was feeling compassion for me. That was the last thing I expected." I explain to him. "He somehow has developed feelings for me, and he is disgusted with what Ansen has done and what he wants to do to me. When you checked on me and asked if I was still alright, I could feel him praying for you to stay in the hallway. Without speaking, he begged me to not give him away because he didn't want to hurt me."

James takes my hand from his face and squeezes it affectionately as he leans down and kisses my cheek.

"What happens to me?" I ask him dumbfounded. "I have no other family!"

"Part of my requirements for taking on a client who is a minor and the parent is in danger is that I must be given guardianship of that child in the case that parent is killed or cannot be found," James explains to me. "

"So as of right now, you have custody of me," I confirm.

"Yes, kiddo." He caresses my cheek. "You have me. You will always have me."

"Good." I lean my face into his hand and smile at him affectionately.

IVAN

I wake up in Rafe's arms the next morning, still dressed in my school uniform and he in his. We are in the guest bedroom and I vaguely remember sobbing while he held me comfortingly last night after I viewed the video Quinn O'Shea gave me.

Since Rafe is still sleeping I lie there and think about the video. Dad isn't my real father and he has known this for a long time. He planned on hurting me as revenge for my mother. Who is my real father and why didn't Mom tell me about him?

I can see now why Nadia asked Rafe if my DNA kit had been picked up. The results of that test hold my future in its hands.

"Hey," Rafe whispers, his voice is groggy. "You're thinking woke me up."

"Sorry." I kiss him on the cheek.

"I wasn't lecturing you." He explains as he yawns widely. "You are already stressing, and you just woke up."

"The video was telling the truth," I tell him. "I have a lot of unanswered questions now. This is why Grams wanted to be sure my DNA kit went out right away."

"Yep." Rafe agrees as he rolls over and strokes a finger across my cheek tenderly. "No matter who your father is you have us and James. You do know the man loves you like you are his own daughter, don't you?"

"Yes." I smile just thinking about James. I look up into Rafe's gorgeous gray eyes as his expression turns seductive. He kisses me, softly at first and then demandingly, while I clutch him tightly, pulling him closer.

A knock at the door breaks us apart and Rafe groans with frustration and when I look over, I see James poking his head in. When he sees what he interrupted he smiles brightly.

"Perfect timing!" He chuckles at Rafe's frustrated expression. "Breakfast will be ready soon and there is a fresh pot of coffee brewing."

He closes the door and I reluctantly slide out of bed to take a change of clothes into the bathroom down the hall. Rafe, I assume, retreats to his bedroom to change out of his school uniform before going downstairs. I brush my teeth, wash my face, and braid my hair after changing into a pair of leggings and a t-shirt.

I am the last person to make it into the kitchen and walk to the coffee pot to pour myself a large mug of coffee. I add cream and sugar before joining everyone at the breakfast table.

"Good morning kiddo." James kisses me on the top of the head

"Good morning." I yawn sheepishly.

We all sit around the table and sip our coffee while Monique finishes cooking breakfast. Due to the large numbers of FBI agents that are still in the house, she and Victoria are cooking pancakes, scrambled eggs, and sausage links. I feel bad that I am not helping them, but they insist that I sit and enjoy my coffee.

After everyone has eaten their fill Dimitri and James pull Rafe and me into the office to discuss some things.

"We have to be in family court tomorrow to discuss my guardianship in front of the judge," James informs me. "I don't expect any problems with it. The house you and Ansen have been living in belongs to one of the men he was supposed to open a practice with, so we can't stay there anymore now that he is missing. My aunt left me a house on St. Charles just a few blocks from here. It has a nice sized yard and we should be able to move in there tonight."

"What about school?" I ask, terrified at the thought of returning there.

"I thought it would be wise for you to homeschool, at least for now," James explains. "We don't have to have the school on lockdown in the hopes of catching O'Shea for nothing."

"You didn't get him, did you?" I ask him dejectedly.

"I'm sorry kiddo, we didn't." James states. "He paid off one of the cafeteria staff to let him in the building last night. We still aren't sure how he made it off of school grounds without us seeing him."

"You don't have to be sorry," I tell him honestly. "I know you would give your life to save mine."

I look into his eyes with the thought of sharing just how much I do love him, and I see him tear up.

"Would you like to go and take a look at our house?" James asks. I stop myself from crying when I hear him call it our house. I nod with an excited smile.

Rafe and Victoria ride along with us as we drive the fourteen blocks over to the house on St. Charles Avenue. It is a white Victorian mansion with black shutters that has a porch with columns gracing it on the first and second floors. The yard is very large and has a very tall stockade privacy fence surrounding the entire property. There is a three-stall garage in the rear next to a patio area with tables and umbrellas.

The inside of the house is mainly polished wood floors, high ceilings with numerous fireplaces, antique furniture, expensive carpets, stained glass windows, and chandeliers. The kitchen is really the only room that has marble floors and modern appliances.

There are five bedrooms and six bathrooms in the large house, way too much room for just James and me. He tells me that I can have my pick of the bedrooms as long as I don't mind the possibility of sharing it with a pet.

"A pet?" I ask, holding my breath hoping he isn't kidding.

"I have a pet that I have had to have cared for while I am on the job. Now that you and I will be living here Ivan can finally come home." James explains.

"Ivan?" I say excitedly. "What kind of a pet is Ivan?"

"Come and take a look," James says with an indifferent shrug although I can feel his need to please me. He leads me out back to what looks like a garage. Inside the building is a large indoor pen where a large black wolf is pacing anxiously.

I instantly kneel down next to the fence and gaze at the male wolf breathlessly as he comes to a stop right in front of me. The wolf and I gaze into each other's eyes curiously.

"He's magnificent." I breathe in awe. Ivan steps right up to the fence and smells the hand that I offer to him.

"I thought you might like him after I saw you at the zoo with that tiger," James says.

"I wanted to set the tiger free," I state as I gaze at Ivan eagerly. "How did you come to have Ivan?"

"I found him as a pup in Canada a couple years ago," James explains. "His mother had been killed in a trap and he was the only remaining pup."

"He's beautiful," I whisper as Ivan lets me stroke his ears. One would almost think that Ivan was a black German shepherd because black wolves are really rather rare. His gold eyes are very vivid, and I can see that he is very intelligent.

"I think he likes you too," Victoria says.

James opens the pen and after Ivan briefly nudges James, he comes up to me and leans his head on my stomach. I kneel down in front of the wolf and communicate my love and acceptance of him as I gaze lovingly into his eyes.

"I have hired movers to take care of everything for us," James tells me as we make our way back into the house with Ivan right at my side. "You need only tell them which bedroom you want, and they will set up your furniture."

"Will you help me pick out a bedroom?" I ask Victoria, knowing she will be totally excited to be given that chore. She squeals eagerly and yanks me back into the house with Ivan keeping pace with us barking all the way.

Victoria walks through each of the five bedrooms, including the master, and thoughtfully looks at the colors before she makes a decision. She doesn't listen to me when I insist that I won't take the master bedroom away from James, even though I know he would let me have it. Thankfully, she likes the bedroom with the silvery walls with the white trim. The moldings along the ceiling and floor are beautifully carved as well as the white marble fireplace. The thick plush carpeting is white, and I have two gold chandeliers hanging from the ceiling with matching gold draperies on the tall windows. The room is sort of long and narrow instead of square.

Victoria drags one of the moving men up to my bedroom and instructs him on where to put the bed, desk, mirrored chest of drawers, and other miscellaneous furniture. Apparently, the moving truck is already here with all of my bedroom furniture from the other house that Ansen bought for me.

Victoria and I retreat down to the kitchen to raid the fridge for something to drink while James and Rafe are busy helping the moving men set up the furniture. Most of the rooms in the house already have furniture and I am guessing that either his aunt left it all to him or he already had most of the house set up, except for the extra bedrooms, which are empty.

We wander into the living room, plop down on the sofa, and turn on the television thrilled to see that the cable is already on. Ivan lies down at my feet after having followed me around everywhere. I can feel Ivan's need to protect me already even though we just met. The wolf can feel my tension and fear so that has put him on alert to make sure I stay safe.

Victoria looks around with a very secretive look on her face before she turns to me eagerly.

"So, tell me about Quinn." She asks, concern and interest obvious on her face. I look around also before I scoot closer to her so we can whisper privately.

"I am a horrible person," I confess to her and then hang my head, wondering how I am supposed to tell her.

"No, you're not!" She exclaims in a quiet tone. "Why?"

"My initial reaction to him when I saw him," I mumble, shame flooding me and making me blush a deep crimson.

"You thought he was attractive!" Victoria breathes in amazement. "Weren't you afraid he was going to slit your throat?"

"No." I shake my head as I look up at her with a tear falling from the corner of my eye. "He was praying to himself that I do not do anything stupid to make him hurt me."

"You feel guilty for your thought because it might hurt Rafe." Victoria guesses correctly. I nod as more tears begin to fall.

She pulls me into a hug and squeezes me tightly until I get control of my emotions.

"You can't help who you think is cute Journee." She lectures me sternly. "Rafe isn't the jealous type anyway and besides it's not like Rafe would ever lose you to Quinn because you would never willingly choose a mob boss over my brother."

"Who am I not jealous of?" Rafe asks as he steps into the room quietly. I feel like a deer caught in headlights as I stare at him in terror that he will be furious with me. I hang my head in shame as Rafe comes over to sit next to me. I can feel his tender touch in my mind to see what I am feeling.

"Baby, you have no reason to be afraid of how I will react to whatever this is." Rafe encourages me gently.

"I thought Quinn was attractive." I blurt in a tiny voice.

Rafe tips up my chin and smiles at me with all of his love visible on his face.

"Does the mob boss have a chance of winning my girl's heart?" He asks me seriously. I shake my head at him as fresh tears course down my face sadly.

"I must be demented to think a guy is hot when he is holding a knife to my throat," I confess.

"I can go with that." Rafe teases me as he kisses me on the forehead. I lean into him and cuddle into his chest with a sigh.

"I don't deserve you," I tell him.

"Yes, you do." He argues with me. "James says that you think Quinn has feelings for you."

"Yeah," I confess. "It was really weird because I could feel a whole lot of compassion, he was feeling for me. I was expecting to be overloaded with all of these violent negative emotions, but there weren't any until he was thinking about Ansen. It is very important to Quinn that he save me from Ansen."

"Doesn't he realize that he is going to be taking you away from all of the people that you love if he manages to abduct you?" Rafe states logically. "Only crazy people think a complete stranger reciprocates love."

"I agree." I sigh. "Enough about Quinn. I pray that I never have to see him again."

Rafe takes time to explain to me about all of the safety features that James already has installed on the property. There is a state of art home security system already in place. There is a room in the garage where a guard will be placed around the clock where he watches all of the camera surveillance that is set up for the perimeter, outside the house. There are also cameras inside the house, but they are watched from inside the house. In addition to the cameras, there are motion sensors in place so that any blind spots are covered.

Until Quinn is caught James will have two men walking the fence line at all times fully armed. Ivan has his doggy door installed in the rear of the house so he can come and go as he pleases.

I get up from the couch and head out of the room, just wanting a few minutes to myself.

"Do you want company?" Victoria asks.

"No. I just need a few minutes." I shake my head as I leave the room with Ivan at my side.

I wander from room to room looking at the décor of each room, the furniture, and the architecture, and just clear my mind and allow myself to feel at peace. Being away from people is a real necessity for an empath because of the constant emotional overload, even if you know how to turn it off.

I really like this house so much better than the mini castle. This one is still considered a mansion, but it is homey and cozy where the other one was like some sort of royal museum that you couldn't relax in.

I like that the bedroom Victoria chose for me is right next to the master bedroom, so I won't be far from James. Even if I just have a nightmare, he is close enough to come and comfort me.

I finally end up curled up on the bed that is completely set up with Ivan right next to me.

FAMILY

I spend most of the day on Wednesday online getting my homeschooling set up and ordering whatever supplies I will need. I am really hoping that I can just complete high school ahead of time just to get it out of the way so I can start college sooner.

I spend all morning taking tests so that they can determine which classes are necessary and where I will start in each one. After taking all of the tests I am glad that I was in a lot of advanced placement classes because I actually test out of all my tenth-grade classes. I have an even mixture of eleventh and twelfth-grade classes that I have to take. I opt out of any extracurricular classes so that I can finish earlier.

By the time it is nearing dinner I am finally finished with all of my homeschooling stuff and I am disappointed that I will have to wait a week for my supplies to arrive before I can get started.

James has been busy all day, no doubt working with Dimitri trying to determine where Quinn is. I take Ivan outside for a while so he can run around the yard and stretch his muscles after sitting in my room most of the day. I tried a couple times to just leave him outside, but he ultimately came in his doggy door to return to my side.

I have had guards around me all day long and I haven't been alone, but it has been a long lonely day.

"Are we going to eat dinner together?" I shoot a text to James hopefully. I can cook myself something to eat, but I miss James.

"I am on my way home kiddo."

I smile happily and can't wait for him to get home. Heading back inside I go back up to my bedroom and take a shower and change into a pair of leggings and a sweatshirt since the temperatures are cooling down. When I head down to the kitchen, I see that not only is James home but Victoria and Rafe are there as well. With a squeal of joy, I throw myself into Rafe's arms and kiss him on the lips in front of everyone. He returns my kiss rather chastely even though I can feel his passion just roaring under the surface.

"I'm happy to see you too baby," Rafe whispers into my ear as he embraces me tightly.

After Rafe releases me I hug Victoria happily too before curling myself into James' chest with a sigh.

"I missed you today," I tell him sincerely.

"I missed you too." He strokes my hair softly. "Did you get all of your homeschooling stuff finished?"

"Yep." I nod with a smile. "Although I can't really get started until all my supplies get here next week. What is that wonderful smell?" I ask as I look at all of the take-out bags on the counter.

"I stopped at my favorite place and picked up some gumbo, jambalaya, and some cornbread," James says as he licks his lips excitedly.

"It looks like you could feed an army," I state as I look at all the containers spread over the island.

"Well, there had to be enough to feed both me and Rafe ya know." James shrugs. "Big guys with big appetites."

We all dig in and gather around the kitchen table to chat while we eat. I look around at everyone and can't believe that a week ago I was still in Seattle and had no idea I was moving to New Orleans. So much has happened in such a short time and my life is totally and completely different now.

I had my friend Nicole in Seattle, so I wasn't exactly lonely, but I guess I didn't realize how much more I have here in New Orleans. Dad, I mean Ansen, was always busy with work and even though he seemed to try and spend time with me I spent most of my time either alone or at Nicole's house.

I have been sending Nicole long emails keeping her up to date on all of the stuff happening around here because I don't want to lose her as a friend. She says that she is glad I found Rafe, an empath just like me, and is devastated about what happened with Ansen.

Victoria is a totally different girl than Nicole, but I couldn't really love her any less. Nicole is outdoorsy and loves being in sports while Victoria could not possibly be any more of a girly girl.

Thanksgiving comes and goes as I settle into my new life with James. Ansen has just completely disappeared leaving no trace as to where he could have gone. There is no financial breadcrumbs, his passport has not been used, and he has not contacted anyone he knows.

Quinn O'Shea is in the wind as well. He has not returned to his home base of Seattle and he nor his men have been seen around New Orleans either. I have not been contacted or have seen Quinn at all.

Life is returning to some semblance of normalcy for me as James and I adjust to life together. We had to appear before the judge so that James has legal rights as my guardian with Ansen being missing.

After four weeks with nothing out of the ordinary happening, James and I have relaxed our guard a bit. I have to admit it is really rather nice to not be terrified daily.

I have managed to already complete one of my eleventh-grade classes in the last four weeks and have moved on to another one of my twelfth-grade classes. James keeps himself busy every day working with the FBI to locate both Ansen and Quinn O'Shea, so I spend almost every day doing homework.

After school most days Victoria and Rafe come over to hang out with me and Ivan. The four of us, yes including the wolf, have grown very close these last few weeks. Victoria and I have gotten to the point where we can finish each other's sentences. Rafe and I are inseparable. I have learned that with Rafe I can be telepathic. It seems that since Rafe is also an empath we can communicate with each other just by thought. We even learned that we can do this from a distance apart. He can be lying in his bed fifteen blocks away and we can carry on a private conversation.

The first Saturday in December arrives and Rafe, Victoria, and I have plans to do some Christmas shopping together. They are already late as it is nearing nine o'clock and I am starting to get hungry for breakfast since we were planning on having beignets at Café du Monde.

James is drinking coffee and watching me impatiently pace the kitchen. When Ivan starts to whine at my whirling emotions James finally speaks up.

"Will you sit down kiddo?" He asks. "What's up?"

"They are late and it's not like them not to text me or something," I explain as I plop down at the table. "I haven't been able to access Rafe's thoughts for hours."

"Have you tried calling the house?" James suggests logically.

I take his suggestion and Monique picks up the phone when I call sounding like she has a cold, or she has been crying. Not wanting to pick at her thoughts I attempt to not pry, although it is really hard.

"I was just wondering if Rafe and Victoria were still coming over today to go Christmas shopping," I state, trying not to sound impatient.

"I think you and James should come over here, Journee," Monique tells me and I can hear from the tone of her voice something is seriously wrong.

"Alright." I agree. "We will be right over."

James puts Ivan in the pen in the garage just to keep him contained in case something was to go wrong. We make the short drive over to the Antonescu home and I feel instantly terrified when I see two police cars parked out front. James and I exchange a look and he shrugs to let me know that he isn't aware of what is going on. I feel a little bit better because I hope that means it isn't anything related to Quinn O'Shea.

Inside the house we find Victoria on the couch cuddled up to her dad, her face tear-stained with dark circles under her eyes. Rafe is furiously pacing back and forth like a caged animal and I can feel his need to do violence. Monique looks like she has been crying as much as Victoria and I can feel her grief from across the room.

James and I sit down on the sofa sectional and look at everyone questioningly.

"You knew I was helping Clare with the Christmas dance preparations at school last night?" Victoria asks in a hoarse voice.

I nod at her and wait for her to continue.

"There was a basketball game last night at the school too. Well, I went to use the same bathroom that you did, back by the band room? Heath was waiting for me in there." Victoria says and then drops her gaze to her lap and begins to sob uncontrollably. I peek into her thoughts to save her the pain of having to repeat her story out loud once more and feel sick at the vivid images of Victoria's rape at the hands of Heath.

He kept repeating to Victoria as he brutally hurt her that it was all Journee's fault that he had to take his revenge like that. He left her bleeding and traumatized on the bathroom floor.

My gaze meets Rafe's and I can feel that he doesn't blame me for this, but I sure do. If I had just kept my mouth shut none of this would have happened.

Grams steps out of the kitchen with a cup of tea in her hand and looks at me with a kind smile.

"Don't you dare take this on, Journee," Grams says. "Heath is a predator and he was hurting girls before you moved here. Victoria will do what is necessary to see that he is put away."

Tears are flowing unchecked down my face as Victoria walks over to me and gives me a halfhearted smile. I pull her into my arms and hold her tenderly, sharing with her mind as much comfort and love as I can.

"It's not your fault," Victoria whispers into my ear. "I will be alright."

"It should have been me," I whisper back. "I am the one he wanted revenge on."

Victoria and I sit down together on the sofa and I listen while Dimitri informs me that Heath was arrested last night and is already out on bail. The police are interviewing other girls from the school in the hopes that others will come forward now that Victoria is testifying to put him away for good. Heath's parents have already contacted Dimitri and Monique in the hopes that they will accept a payment to keep quiet because they want their boy to have his basketball scholarship. Victoria's parents refused the money of course and even bluntly told Heath's parents that he has hurt enough innocent girls.

"Was a rape kit done at the hospital?" I ask. "Were fluids collected?"

"Yes." Dimitri nods with a sigh. "They collected Heath's DNA to compare to what was found on the rape kit. Results should be just a day or two."

"Your DNA came back," Victoria tells me as she attempts to smile at me.

"We can worry about that later," I state, knowing Victoria is more important right now.

"I would really love something else to focus on right now." Victoria states with a sigh. "I am done thinking about Heath. Do you need me for anything else?" Victoria asks her dad.

"No princess." He smiles at her affectionately.

"Can Rafe and I go spend the weekend with Journee and James?" Victoria asks in a very subdued voice.

"Of course." Both Monique and Dimitri chorus at the same time.

"It will do you good to get away for a couple days," Monique says with a weary smile.

I follow Victoria upstairs and help her pack an overnight bag while I desperately try not to tear up anymore at the thought of my dear friend suffering because of me. This is all my fault!

'It's not your fault baby.' Rafe's comforting drawl resonates through my thoughts.

'I have never wanted to hurt someone before, and I swear I want to kill Heath.' I confess to Rafe, feeling shame for the strong need for violence rushing through me.

'Me too!' Rafe agrees. *'We need to be there for Victoria in any way that she wants us. We will all heal from this eventually.'*

Victoria is extremely quiet which worries me a lot, but I let her have her privacy because I know it is something that she needs right now. James is ready to go by the time me, Victoria, and Rafe make it downstairs. Victoria hugs both of her parents and my heart just goes out to her.

As soon as James lets Ivan out of his pen in the garage the wolf makes a beeline for Victoria, even climbing up on my bed next to her to lie his head on her lap.

I can feel Ivan's turmoil as he senses Victoria's roiling emotions and his need to comfort her. Victoria curls up next to Ivan and promptly falls asleep.

James is downstairs making breakfast for all of us so Rafe and I just curl up on the big bed by Victoria to be nearby in case she has a nightmare. I peek into her mind while she lies there sleeping and she is so exhausted from not sleeping last night that her thoughts are clear.

Rafe and I just cuddle up together on the bed and just enjoy being close to one another while we keep an eye on Victoria. James comes in after an hour or so to let us know that breakfast is ready and Rafe has to practically drag me from the room.

"You can listen to her thoughts from the kitchen," Rafe explains to me as he pulls me into the hallway. "See? Ivan won't leave her either. He will be in the room with her to protect her too."

"Besides, you need to eat something." James insists with a sad smile. "I won't let you waste away because you can't eat when you are stressed."

As soon as I walk into the kitchen my stomach grumbles at the smells of sausage, French toast, scrambled eggs, and freshly brewed coffee. The three of us sit around the kitchen table and eat heartily.

I clean up the kitchen while the guys sit and chat as they sip their coffee. Keeping myself partially aware of Victoria's thoughts I am still surprised when an image of Heath poised above her appears in her mind as she starts to toss and turn in her sleep. The plate that I am drying slips out of my hands and crashes to the floor breaking into a million pieces as I run from the room.

Rafe and James rush upstairs with me and I manage to curl myself around Victoria and wake her from her nightmare gently before she starts screaming.

"You're alright," I whisper to her while Ivan paces the bedroom and whines because of the fear he feels coming off of Victoria. She comes awake with a start and hides her face in my chest as shame flows through her.

"Don't!" I murmur to her consolingly. "You have nothing to feel ashamed of!" I rock her soothingly as I hum softly. She clings to me as I comfort her and send feelings of peace into her mind. She stops trembling and slips back to sleep. Ivan hops up on the bed and curls himself around her after I let her go.

Rafe and I sit at my desk where we look over my DNA results on the website that has my tiny family tree. I have a couple of close family matches and one is obviously my biological father and the other could be either a half-sibling or an aunt, considering that she is a girl. When I see which DNA matches are related to my father I see that the girl is not on there so I deduce that she must be related to my mother.

The name of my biological father is Edward Beauvais and it looks like he lives right here in New Orleans. This surprises me because neither Ansen nor I knew where Mom was from specifically. I send him an email explaining who I am and some details about my mom, hoping that he will respond to me. I really try to not get my hopes up that he will even want to meet me let alone invite me into his life.

I also send an email to the girl, Xanthia Dinescu, and pretty much explain the same things to her. Rafe helps me look over my biological father's family tree, but I can only see deceased relatives.

After a few hours, I switch over to my DNA breakdown to see where I come from. I am about sixty-six percent Europe East which includes the countries of Romania where my mother's ancestors came from, and thirty-four percent Europe West and judging from what little research I did on my dad's tree his ancestors came from France. I am Romanian and French.

I am just getting ready to shut down my computer when I get a response from Xanthia Dinescu.

Dearest Journee,

My name is Xanthia and the woman who was your mother, Sasha, was my much older sister. I would love to meet somewhere and have a cup of coffee. I am saddened that she has been gone for so long.

Eagerly awaiting your response.

I reread the email like ten times as it suddenly hits me, I have an aunt! I can feel Rafe's excitement for me as he sits next to me and waits for me to make a decision. I want to meet her and know I will have to discuss this at length with James just to be sure that I am safe.

Leaving my computer on, I motion for Rafe to follow me as I go to look for James and find him in the kitchen finishing up dinner.

"I have an aunt who lives here in New Orleans." I blurt out quickly. "My mother's younger sister and she wants to meet somewhere for coffee. I would love to meet her. Can you tell me what you would like me to do or say to her so that you are comfortable that I am safe?"

James looks at me happily and nods his agreement for me to meet my aunt.

"Let's pick a place where I know the owner and can have a protection detail in place," James tells me thoughtfully. "Café Envie is on Decatur and I think it is a good location to use. Go and email her back and suggest that one. See if she is available tomorrow morning at ten o'clock."

Rafe and I go back upstairs and email my aunt Xanthia. She responds almost immediately that ten o'clock tomorrow morning at the Café Envie is perfect. She includes a picture of herself so that I know who to look for when I arrive at the café.

MEMORIES

I look at my aunt Xanthia's picture and I can see some similarities to my mom, but I am disappointed that she doesn't have our purple eye color. Her hair is a dark brown instead of black, her eyes are a cornflower blue color and her nose is shaped differently, a little longer on the tip than mine. The shape of her face, the slant of her eyes, and her lips are the same as mine and Moms. Of course, since she doesn't have the purple eyes, she has a tan, something I am unable to have with my porcelain skin.

I am disappointed that I can't tell how tall she is because I am quite dainty at only five feet tall, as was Mom. She looks like she has an average build because the width of her shoulders does not look overly petite.

"I think you have her memorized." Rafe chuckles.

"I am so excited," I whisper as Victoria slides off the bed and comes up behind me.

"Who is that?" She asks as she yawns widely.

"It's my mom's younger sister, Xanthia Dinescu," I explain. "She lives here in New Orleans and we are going to meet at Café Envie on Decatur tomorrow morning. I found my biological father too. His name is Edward Beauvais and I sent him an email as well, but he hasn't responded."

"Oh Journee, you must be so totally excited!" Victoria exclaims, sounding a little more like her old self.

"Dinner's ready." James pokes his head into my room with a grin.

We all head down to the kitchen and I get a whiff of beef roast with a rich brown gravy and my stomach growls loudly since I haven't eaten since breakfast.

Rafe, James, and I exchange happy looks as we see Victoria start loading her plate as she licks her lips hungrily. It warms my heart to see that her appetite is back, at least for now.

"Dimitri called this afternoon to let us know that the police have five more girls from school that have given their statements and are willing to testify against Heath." James states after swallowing a big bite of meat. Victoria actually smiles happily at this news.

"Good," Victoria exclaims with a decisive nod. "I hope they find even more so that his family can't buy him out of this one. He enjoys doing this and needs to be stopped before more girls are hurt."

"I have tomorrow morning all set up at Café Envie," James says. "Everyone will be in plain clothes and just look like normal people stopping for coffee on a Sunday morning."

"It might be helpful to you if you have Rafe close to you somewhere or can communicate with him considering that we are telepathic," I suggest to James.

"On top of that kiddo." James nods his agreement. "Rafe will have a two-way radio and we will be out of sight because I am sure Quinn and his goons know what we look like."

"Are you nervous about finding out why your mom never told you about your real dad?" Victoria asks me.

"Completely," I reply with a groan. "As well as why she left behind her sister and possibly her parents. I just want good news because I am so tired of bad news."

"You have to think about this from your aunt's perspective too." Victoria brings to my attention. "She lost her sister and you are a piece of your mom. You just might find an aunt who is so totally excited to have you in her life as well as the possibility of grandparents."

"What would I do without you Victoria?" I ask her sincerely, so grateful to have such a wonderful friend.

"I absolutely love Ivan." Victoria changes the subject with a fond smile at the wolf who is sitting behind her chair. "He would make a wonderful therapy dog."

"He made a beeline for you as soon as he got into the house today," James told her. "He has always refused to leave Journee's side when she is upset also."

Victoria and I clean up the kitchen after dinner while Rafe and James get movies picked out in the living room for the night. We bring pop out into the living room to drink while Rafe starts the first movie, an action flick of course. We spend the evening watching movies, snacking, and joking around.

I insist on Victoria sleeping with me so that I will be close by in case of any nightmares. Ivan sleeps at the foot of the bed as he seems reluctant to leave her just yet.

The early morning sunshine wakes me up and I look over at the other pillow expecting to see Victoria still asleep, but she is gone. Ivan is missing as well, and I can guarantee that they are together somewhere.

After brushing my hair and my teeth I make my way downstairs to the kitchen to find Victoria sipping a cup of coffee on the patio. I join her with my own mug of sweetened coffee and watch Ivan running around trying to catch a seagull.

"How did you sleep last night?" I ask her.

"Better." She tells me with a sigh. "Not one nightmare."

"Are you going to be ok?" I ask her seriously.

"Oh sure." She nods firmly. "Mom messaged me and says that she has me set up to see a psychiatrist and I think I will join a support group."

"Wow," I exclaim. "I think I would be in shambles still and you already have everything all planned out."

"It helps me to stay focused and not completely lose my sanity." She says. "I want to just curl up in a ball and cry, never go to school again, and just hide away in my bedroom forever."

"I hope he goes away for the rest of his life," I state.

"I want to help other girls like me," Victoria says in a soft voice. "I can't decide if I want to become an attorney so I can prosecute the rapists or become some sort of a therapist who helps the victims."

"You would be good at both," I tell her seriously. "You have a way of really seeing into a person and notice things others don't. You are also stubborn and determined enough to be an attorney."

"She is definitely stubborn enough." Rafe teases her as he takes a seat at the patio table.

"With a brother like you, it came in handy," Victoria states airily.

Rafe leans over the table and gives me one of those seductive glances so I lean forward, and we kiss briefly to not gross-out Victoria.

"I'm going to go take a shower and decide what to wear." I make my way back into the house with Ivan at my heels again. Apparently, Victoria must be feeling good enough that Ivan doesn't feel the need to stay with her.

After my shower, I dry my hair before walking into my closet and look at everything critically. I really want my aunt to like me and I know what I wear really doesn't matter, but I want it to be perfect. The weather is supposed to be unseasonably warm, so I look over my dresses and finally decide on a white and pink one with spaghetti straps and a fitted bodice. The skirt flares down over my hips and stops a couple inches above my knees. It's made of rayon and feels good against my skin. A silver necklace and bracelets with white flats complete my outfit. I apply some light-colored eye shadow and some mascara before looking at myself uncertainly.

"You're perfect," Victoria reassures me from the doorway. "Rafe will think so too."

"Are you sure this outfit is alright?" I ask her nervously. Victoria laughs brightly.

"Yes. I think it is adorable." She reassures me again. "James and Rafe are ready."

We walk downstairs and find the guys in the foyer discussing details about watching me at the café. It is just ten o'clock when I step into the café and look around for my aunt. She is sitting in a corner by the far window and already has a cup of something in front of her.

I order a mocha latte and then walk over to her table with a nervous smile.

"Aunt Xanthia?" I ask, my heart pounding quickly. She looks up at me and her face pales slightly before she smiles. She gets to her feet and pulls me into her arms tightly.

"You look exactly like I remember your mother the last time I saw her." Aunt Xanthia says.

Aunt Xanthia is about half a foot taller than me and is curvier than I am with an athletic build. She releases me with a sheepish smile and sits back down. I sit across from her and return her smile, so thrilled that she already seems to accept me as family.

"Do you know anything about Sasha's life here in New Orleans?" My aunt asks me. I shake my head at her sadly.

"Until I found you yesterday, I didn't even know she was from here," I confess. "Do you know my real father, Edward Beauvais?"

"I was six when your mom disappeared so a lot of the information I have I had to ask my parents about." She tells me. "Our family has been a part of New Orleans society for generations and growing up in society my parents had certain expectations of your mom. They arranged a marriage for her with another family from that same society of peers, your father; Edward Beauvais. He was the same age as your mom, and they knew each other but I don't think Sasha would have ever gone out with him. She wanted to please our parents, so she agreed to the marriage until one day she just disappeared. We never heard from her again. Are you for certain that Edward Beauvais is your biological father?"

"Yes." I nod, trying to absorb everything she told me. "I found him on the website I did my DNA through."

"Have you tried to get a hold of him yet?" Aunt Xanthia asks.

"I sent him an email at the same time as yours," I tell her. "He hasn't responded yet."

"I don't think he will respond, at least not right away anyway." She shares with me honestly. "I was told he was furious that your mom ran away. He got married about four years later and he has a young teenage daughter."

"I have a half-sister," I whisper in awe. "I had never even thought of that."

"I know you are probably eager to meet him and make a connection. I just wanted to encourage you to give him time to realize you exist." She reasons with me. "What happened with the guy that your mom married?"

"He disappeared," I whisper, ashamed. "It's a long depressing story."

"Who are you living with?" She asks, instantly concerned.

"A wonderful guy who is an ex-navy seal," I tell her with a smile. "My stepfather hired him as a bodyguard for me. He is my legal guardian. Do you know where the bathroom is?" I ask her as I look around and don't see any signs. She points to the hallway next to the cash register.

"Take that hallway all the way down and around the corner." She explains. "It's behind the kitchen."

I am reaching for the women's bathroom door when I am snatched from behind and pulled into a different room. I am pushed up against a wall with a hand over my mouth and when I look up, I see Quinn O'Shea smiling down at me again. I shake my head and before I can even squirm, he leans his body weight against mine until I can barely breathe.

He holds up his cell phone and on it, I can see my best friend Nicole with a knife to her throat. Quinn releases my mouth but pins my wrists above my head with one hand while he keeps the cell phone visible with the other.

"She's a bonny lass, yer friend Nicole." Quinn's thick Irish brogue washes over me. "If I doona get back to her they will be forced to keep her. No notifying anyone we are having this little chat, aye?"

I nod my agreement and try to keep my emotions under control in case Rafe decides to check on me. Dismissing my initial panic to reach out and communicate telepathically with Rafe I pray Quinn isn't planning on taking me with him right now.

"Ye doona remember me do ye lass?" He asks seriously.

Remember him? I shake my head in confusion.

"Ye were about ten years old and Ansen came to see Connor. Some of the lads were teasing ye about being so tiny. One of them was going to hurt ye." Quinn shares with me as he watches my expression carefully.

The memory comes to me when I peek into his thoughts and see the visual in his mind of the events he described.

"A guy named Declan protected me," I remember as I look up at him, curious as to why this is important to him and then I remember; Connor was his brother! He must have been there, but I cannot remember a guy named Quinn. I had the biggest crush on Declan after that. My knight in shining armor came to my rescue with the sexy accent. Declan was the reason I started to notice boys at ten years old.

It was six years ago, and the details of his face have faded a bit but as I study Quinn's face it suddenly hits me; Quinn is Declan. All color drains from my cheeks as I come to this realization. Quinn remembers me fondly and knew I had an infatuation with him. He doesn't seriously think I still feel that way? I was a child!

"Aye, now ye remember." Quinn's voice grows huskier as he nuzzles my ear.

"I will give ye a week." He whispers into my ear. "Ye will meet me in St. Louis Cathedral Friday night at midnight or yer friend Nicole disappears into a life of prostitution. Doona make the mistake of thinking ye can find her. I want to let her go back to her family, but the decision is yers, Journee."

I simply stare at him, unable to nod or shake my head as he gazes down at me thoughtfully. He brushes his lips across mine softly, not demanding a response or deepening the kiss, just a simple caress.

TRUTH?

I make my way back to the table my aunt is sitting at, not having to use the bathroom anymore with my mind all awhirl. I know that Rafe has a hard time reading me when there is a bit of a distance between us, but I am attempting to clear my thoughts and I am really struggling to control my emotions.

As I step closer to the table and look at my aunt Xanthia it suddenly occurs to me that she is related to Mom; is she gifted somehow? If she is, I am sure she can already feel my distress as I desperately try to make it disappear with no success.

I peek into her thoughts and feel her brush my thoughts at the same time.

"Are you alright Journee?" She asks, when I know she feels me I slam my mental wall up so she can't read me.

"Please don't ask." I plead with her. "I'm fine. I cannot tell you why I am upset, not right now."

I sit down across from her as I feel a tear slip down my cheek.

"In my excitement, I had completely forgotten that you might be like Mom and me," I confess as I look at her with new eyes. "Are you only an empath like Mom was or like me? I'm telepathic as well." I whisper.

"I'm only an empath." She tells me with a smile. "I wonder where you got your additional abilities from. Your grandmother is telepathic, and your great-grandmother was an empath. I have never heard of anyone in our family having both. How do you handle all of the overload?"

"Mom showed me how to turn it off and just read people selectively. It took me a while to learn how to do it without conscious thought, but now it is just instinct." I explain to her. "Of course, Mom didn't know I was telepathic. I didn't really know until a few weeks ago."

"I want you to know that I am here for you when you are ready to share things with me." Aunt Xanthia tells me. "Your grandparents are eager to meet you."

"Grandparents," I murmur to myself, having forgotten that little detail as well.

Aunt Xanthia laughs at my dumbfounded expression.

"Whenever you are ready." She tells me. "I hate to have to leave you so soon after meeting you, but I have a college thing I have to attend at eleven."

She hands me her cell phone number with a warm smile. She hugs me tightly before she hurries out the door and I get the impression she is always on the go.

After she is gone Rafe joins me at the table and gives me a probing look.

"I felt a brief moment of extreme emotions from you when you left the table." He states as he waits expectantly for my explanation.

"Aunt Xanthia knows who my biological dad is and told me that he most likely won't want anything to do with me because of the way that things ended with my mom," I confess to him honestly and purposely keep my thoughts focused on this topic only.

"Maybe he just needs some time to adjust to the fact that you are his," Rafe explains. "This is probably a great shock to him. If Ansen thought that you were his daughter for years, then he must have met your mother when she was barely pregnant with you."

"I guess I hadn't thought of it that way." I muse thoughtfully. "Let's go home."

I grab my mocha and follow Rafe from the café and force myself not to look around for Quinn. My heart is breaking for the fear that Nicole must be going through right now, and I pray that she remains untouched until I can get there.

Rafe can feel my distress and I know he is thinking it is due to my real father and I let him think this. He holds my hand in his and gives it a tender squeeze as we ride with James back to the house.

Victoria has made a big breakfast and wants to know all the details of my meeting with my aunt. I fill her in on everything except for my run-in with Quinn. She thinks it is exciting that I found a family that is gifted like I am because she believes it will help bond us that much quicker.

I excuse myself to go outside and sit in the garden with Ivan so I can have some privacy to think alone. I curl up in a ball and Ivan nudges the front of my legs and whines at me plaintively because he wants to help. I allow myself to cry as I think about leaving behind all of the people that I have grown to love as well as leaving behind a family I have just found before I even get a chance to meet them. As I am sitting there feeling sorry for myself, I hear a strange whizzing sound right about the same time that Ivan yelps and falls over. I slide to the ground and see an arrow protruding from his rib cage while Ivan bleeds from his mouth.

"Rafe!" I yell to my boyfriend telepathically. *"Ivan has been shot with an arrow."*

Within seconds James, Rafe, and Victoria are crowded around me and Ivan while I stroke his ears and cry. Ivan's heart stops beating, and he is gone making me wail my grief like a madwoman.

A couple of minutes later while I am cradling Ivan to me and sobbing a couple of our guards walk up with Heath held between them. Heath is holding a bow with a quiver of arrows the same color as the one still stuck inside Ivan. James calls the police as Rafe hurries Victoria into the house away from Heath.

"I was aiming for you! Stupid bitch!" Heath hisses at me venomously while he struggles to free himself from the guards holding him tightly. I shake my head at him as I cradle Ivan.

"You really aren't very intelligent are you Heath?" I state bitterly. James instructs the guards to take Heath into the study inside the house to wait for the police to arrive.

"Well, now the boy will go away for attempted murder," James states incredulously as he leans down next to me and strokes Ivan's head tenderly. A tear slides down his face and I can feel the grief emanating from him at Ivan's death. He snaps the arrow in half, so it doesn't protrude very far before he picks him up and heads for the garage.

He lies Ivan down in his pen on the blanket that is there and wraps him in it softly. I reluctantly follow James back into the house and wash the blood off of my hands in one of the main floor bathrooms.

Victoria and Rafe step up to me and both hug me to let me know they are there for me. Knowing I have to leave with Quinn on Friday and now losing Ivan in addition to knowing that my biological father doesn't want me is too much for me.

I break away from them and rush upstairs to change out of my soiled clothes and take a long hot shower. I put on some comfortable running clothes and intend on slipping out through the garage so I can be alone. The need is just overwhelming, and I cannot ignore it.

Knowing that James and Rafe will not allow me out of the house I sneak down a back hallway hoping to use the unused back servant door. I am near the door with all of my senses on high alert, even paying attention to stray thoughts when I hear Rafe thinking nearby.

"I really hope that Heath doesn't say something he will regret."

I want to pause to find out what in the world he is thinking about but my need to be alone is stronger. Why would he worry about what Heath has to say and why would he want him to keep quiet?

I slip out the back door silently and walk to the garage which fronts onto the sidewalk with a door that has an alarm on it. I am praying the guard in the garage doesn't stop me to ask where I am going and why I don't have someone along to protect me.

When I run around the corner, I hop on a trolley that is heading towards the big park that the Audubon Zoo is in, just needing the peace that comes from nature.

I am deep in the park and sitting on the ground next to a small pond when I feel someone approaching from behind me, I turn and feel instantly threatened when I see it is Quinn.

"Yer safe lass." He holds up his hands nonthreateningly. "I saw what happened to the wolf. I wanted to make sure ye were alright."

I really don't want to show vulnerability in front of him, but as I gaze up into his face, I cannot help but remember my Declan. I dig right into his head to see what his true intentions are for following me here and all I can find is worry and compassion for me. That is all I have ever found when I have inspected his thoughts. I'm so confused. I motion to the ground next to me with my hand and he sits down next to me.

"The guy who killed Ivan was aiming for me," I whisper as I gaze out at the water, still trying to make sense of everything.

"Aye. Ye stopped him from doing what he loves." Quinn explains gently.

"Why are you trying to force me to come to you?" I ask him bluntly, feeling free to question him considering how laid back he feels.

"Ye already know the answer to that question Journee." He replies as he looks at me thoughtfully.

"You think you are protecting me from Ansen, but he is already gone and no longer a threat to me." I protest angrily.

"He is not the only threat to ye lass." His Irish accent turns mournful.

"You?" I exclaim furiously. "I had half of the country FBI agents on standby to keep you away from me. Everyone is telling me how dangerous you are."

"Then why are ye no running away from me Journee?" Quinn questions me honestly. Stunned, I can only stare at him dumbfounded.

"I can feel goodness in you," I whisper as a tear slips down my face. "I'm confused. Why don't you tell me who is a threat to me?"

Before I realize what is happening, I am on my back and Quinn is reclining over me slightly with my wrists above my head in one of his hands. As he smiles down at me, I see another glimpse of my Declan and my heart softens just a bit.

"Ye winnae believe me." He murmurs, his husky accent giving me goosebumps. "I have to let ye see for yerself."

Quinn's expression turns heated as he just gazes down at me and watches my reaction to him. I can tell that he feels my acceptance of him, but his expression remains the same and he doesn't lower his head to kiss me. He doesn't attempt to rub in that I am attracted to him either.

I think about Rafe and instantly feel guilty for allowing myself to have feelings for someone else, so I blush before looking away from Quinn. I should be ashamed of myself.

Quinn is reluctant, but he rolls away before he helps me to sit up.

"James will be worried lass." He pulls me to my feet. "Ye should go home."

"Seriously?" I look at him in amazement.

"Aye lass." Quinn cocks his head to the side. "Havena I always told ye I would protect ye? I'm yer Declan. Remember that."

Quinn disappears into the trees until I can't see him anymore, but I know he is still keeping an eye on me. I walk back through the park to the trolley stop and obediently head home, my mind full of confusing thoughts.

I felt an instant connection to Rafe because he is an empath just like me, but I also feel a connection to Quinn that I just can't deny to myself any longer. Plus, what was with that thought I caught Rafe thinking about Heath before I left the house? What did he mean by that and why would he care what Heath said? It is definitely something I am going to have to investigate without Rafe noticing.

A black luxury car with tinted windows drives past me slowly as I approach the back door to the garage. I am pretty convinced that it is my Declan making sure I got home alright. For some strange reason, this makes me smile.

As soon as I walk into the house Rafe stalks up to me furiously, his body tense with his fists clenched.

"Where have you been?" He demands instantly before I can even greet him.

I raise my eyebrow at him and just look at him without speaking as I cannot believe he actually expects me to answer to him. I see James and Victoria step up behind Rafe and I am aware that he doesn't know they are there yet.

"I asked you a question Journee." Rafe's voice softens, but I feel the aggression behind it which throws me off guard. I very softly look deeply into his thoughts, so he doesn't know I am in there while I smile at him belligerently.

"How long have we known each other Rafe?" I ask him in deceptively soft tones.

While I am digging around in his thoughts, I catch a brief glimpse of Rafe with Heath and a girl before he slams a wall down, effectively blocking my investigation. I have no idea what was happening between the three of them, but I felt Rafe's eagerness for whatever was about to conspire.

"If you want to know something you only have to ask." Rafe spits out. "You don't need to sneak around in my head without my permission."

I can see Victoria's expression change to distress and confusion at her brother's behavior towards me.

"You and Heath are friends," I state, waiting for him to deny it. He scoffs at me but doesn't deny it. Victoria's face pales to a sickly gray color when her brother doesn't deny my statement. James wraps an arm around her to comfort her when it looks like she will break down in tears.

"Why would you care what Heath tells the police?" I ask him. "Before I left to go on a run you hoped that Heath wouldn't say something that he would regret. What would that be Rafe and why would you care? What was that memory I just saw in your head with you, Heath, and a red-headed girl? You were awfully excited for something to happen before you blocked me from your thoughts."

"Sarah Bryant." Victoria whispers and Rafe swings around with panic all over his face.

"No Victoria!" Rafe practically screams. "That wasn't me!"

While Rafe is busy trying to convince his sister of his innocence I am fishing around in his head again and find the memory of this red-haired girl and Heath. I find it. She is begging Heath to leave her alone and she doesn't know that Rafe is there hidden out of her sight, waiting for his turn.

Instantly nauseous, I barely manage to make it to the bathroom and throw up as I refuse to witness the rest of Rafe's memory. Oh my god, he was helping Heath to rape girls.

I rinse out my mouth quickly and rush back out to share with James what I saw. Rafe is still trying to convince his sister that he had nothing to do with Sarah Bryant and Victoria is sobbing uncontrollably.

"Rafe has been helping Heath to rape the girls at school," I state loudly. "None of the girls will probably be able to identify him because he remained out of their sight."

I turn away and leave the house boldly from the front door and out the front gate without bothering to turn off the alarm. I hear it blaring as I run down the sidewalk in the direction of Jackson Square as fast as I can.

Vaguely, I notice the same black luxury car with the tinted windows keeping pace with me on the road. I am eventually grabbed from behind and even though I struggle I cannot free myself. I peek into the head of the person holding me tightly and feel my Declan. Immediately, I go limp in his arms, and he carries me to his car, placing me in the passenger seat. He takes me to a large plantation that is outside of New Orleans on River Road with a high electric fence and guarded front gate.

The house is a traditional plantation house in white with the columns gracing the front. Without a word, he swings me up in his arms and carries me inside the house and up to the second-floor master suite. He sits down in an overstuffed armchair in front of the fireplace and cradles me on his lap while I dissolve into tears.

My Declan holds me silently while I cry my heart out over Rafe's betrayal. I wanted to give him my virginity before I had to give myself to Quinn. To think of all of those girls that he raped with Heath and I didn't even know he was a monster.

"What happened?" Quinn asks me tenderly when I have finally stopped crying.

"Rafe has been helping Heath rape the girls at school." I share with him without really thinking about how I was supposed to have found this out.

"Ye weren't home vera long lass." He points out.

"No." I agree without saying any more.

"Connor knew yer mum was psychic," Quinn says matter-of-factly. I look up at Quinn in shock and search his expression as I contemplate looking into his mind to see exactly what he knows.

"Aye lass, I know all about yer gift." He tells me. "I figured it out when ye were ten."

"I was still learning about it then," I confess as I blush and look away from him uncertainly.

"Sorry I am about Rafe," Quinn says sincerely. "I know ye thought he was the one when ye found out he was an empath too."

"You really mean that," I reply in awe that how I feel is so important to him.

"I vowed to protect ye the night we met as kids and when ye stood in front of me and declared to all the others there that night that I was yer Declan I figured that meant ye were mine as well," Quinn whispers as he gazes at me heatedly.

Feeling bold for the first time in my life I reach up and pull his head down to mine and brush my lips across his softly. He growls deep in his throat and deepens the kiss quickly, claiming my mouth with his tongue. Bashfully, I kiss him back and suckle his tongue into my mouth.

I peek into his mind and find his overwhelming relief at my acceptance of him, the joy that I instigated our kiss.

"James will be worried Journee," Quinn tells me. "He willnae like ye being with me."

"I'm confused," I whisper.

"I know ye are." He embraces me gently and kisses the top of my head.

MY DECLAN

To my amazement, Quinn takes me directly home without dropping me off a few blocks from my house.

"I can walk in by myself." I insist when it becomes apparent that he wants to walk me inside. "You aren't safe here Quinn."

"Come along lass." He insists calmly and ushers me ahead of him, right into the house without pause.

James rushes out to meet us as soon as he hears us come in. His eyebrow raises questioningly when he sees who I am with before he pulls his gun on him calmly.

"Are you alright kiddo?" James asks me, his heart in his throat. I nod, not really knowing what else to say as the realization of what happened with Rafe hits me again. "You are on the news," James says to Quinn.

"Aye, I am," Quinn replies with a grin. "Please, Quinn is dead now. Call me Declan."

"Why is he bringing you home Journee?" James asks without lowering his weapon.

"I followed her when she ran out of the house and picked her up down the block," Declan answers for me. "I didn't want Ansen to get her."

"Declan doesn't want to hurt me, James." I place myself in front of Declan protectively. "He won't hurt me. Where are Victoria and Rafe?"

"Dimitri took them home," James states as he reluctantly lowers his gun.

James has the news on and as I look up at the television, I see an interview with Quinn. Quinn has declared that he is dismantling the Irish crime syndicate *The Incorporated* that his brother Connor built. All of the young girls who were abducted and sold into prostitution are being returned to their families with the help of the FBI. The numerous strip clubs the syndicate owned all over the country have been shut down for further investigation at the behest of Quinn O'Shea. Warehouses full of guns and drugs have been turned over to the authorities as well.

"What about Nicole?" I ask Declan, still confused. Declan actually blushes and hands me his cell phone.

"She will explain it to ye." Declan states without further explanation. When I open his contact list, I see Nicole as the most frequently contacted person. I raise my eyebrow at him questioningly as I dial her number.

"Did it work?" Nicole's voice demands excitedly from the other end with no greeting whatsoever.

"Did what work?" I ask her curiously. "How is prostitution going for you?"

"Journee! Oh, I'm so happy that you are with Declan. Is everything alright between the two of you? Oh, I knew my idea would work!" Nicole gushes excitedly.

"It was your idea to have Quinn manipulate me to come to him willingly because he was going to sell you on the black market?" I exclaim into the phone furiously. "Do you know how much I cried over you, you little brat?"

"It's Declan, Journee." Nicole lectures me teasingly. "Of course, it was my idea! You were in danger and you wouldn't let him help you and to make matters worse you didn't even remember your knight in shining armor! Your Declan came to save you and you didn't even remember him!"

I blush because Nicole is talking so loudly both Declan and James can hear her.

"I had an FBI agent show me a picture of Declan and tell me his name was Quinn O'Shea. I never knew what Declan's last name was, remember?" I remind her. "The FBI was afraid that Quinn was after me for revenge because it was Ansen's fault that his brother Connor was killed."

"Trust me, there is no love lost between those two brothers." Nicole goes on confidently. "Declan is thrilled to be able to shut down that Irish Mafia thing."

"You know I am furious with you, right?" I ask her seriously.

"Yep, but you love me anyway," Nicole says sassily, confident in our long friendship.

"That psycho empath guy you met at school didn't rape you, did he?" Nicole asks me anxiously.

"No Nicole," I reassure her as a tear slips down my cheek and before I can say any more Declan takes his phone from me.

"Ye need to give the lass some time Nicole." Declan lectures her gently. "She has been through a lot."

I don't hear what Nicole says back to Declan, but he looks satisfied before he hands me the phone back.

"Tell your navy seal guardian that I am coming to stay over Christmas break," Nicole informs me, ever the one to take control.

James just nods his agreement and laughs so hard he has to hold his side.

"I cannot wait to meet the whirlwind that is your friend Nicole." James laughs loudly.

"Good, because I was going to come anyway," Nicole states, having heard what James said. "He couldn't keep me away if he wanted to."

"I can't wait to see you again," I tell her sincerely.

"Me too, Journee." She whispers with a catch in her voice.

After hanging up, I hand the cell phone back to Declan without looking up at him because I am totally embarrassed by what Nicole said. Declan chuckles at my reaction as he puts his phone back in his pocket.

"Nicole is right ye know." Declan's Irish accent thickens with his emotions as he gazes at me affectionately. Reluctantly, I look up at him and get caught in the love for me that is shining in his dark eyes. I nod before blushing some more and looking up at James to see his reaction to all this. He looks like he approves but is debating on whether or not to lay down the law now or wait a little bit.

"Let's sit down so I can explain how Declan and I know each other," I tell James a bit sheepishly. We all sit down on the sofa together with me perched between them while I tell him how Ansen brought me to a meeting with Connor once.

"You felt something for a ten-year-old when you were sixteen," James says to Declan questioningly.

"Not in that way," Declan explains. "Surely, ye have seen her innocent sweetness that ye would give yer life to protect."

"Instantly." James agrees.

"I would have pounded all of those lads for even wanting to hurt her." Declan continues. "When she stood in front of me and innocently declared that I was her Declan I lost my heart to the little kitten who decided to show her claws to a bunch of wolves. I vowed to myself that day I would always protect her."

James' expression changes to show how impressed he is with Declan's confession.

"You just now appeared in her life again." James points out.

"Visibly aye." Declan agrees. "I know everything that happened to her after that day. She needs me now. She was safe before."

"My mom?" I ask him, grief nearly clogging my throat.

"Aye, I knew Ansen killed her, but Connor wouldna help me prove it to the police. I even knew he used a pesticide to cause the high fever, but the body processes it too quickly for it to show up on any testing." Declan tells me sadly.

"Ansen wasna going to hurt ye until ye were closer to be an adult. For the time being, ye were safer living with him." Declan declared. "I was only sixteen and had no way of raising ye without Connor's support and I dinnae want ye raised in the Irish mob."

"How did you know about Rafe when his own family didn't know?" I ask curiously.

"I have had a private detective assigned to ye since ye were ten," Declan informs me. "Anyone that ye have met or associated with has had an extensive background check done on them automatically. When Rafe was a wee fella he did some pretty terrible things and was seeing a psychiatrist who told the Antonescu's that he had no conscience. When Rafe learned how to fool people and pretend to be normal his parents thought he was cured, allowing him to stop seeing that doctor."

"What sort of things had Rafe done?" I ask hesitantly, not sure if I really want to know.

"Set fires inside the house, killed some pets of their neighbors, pushed Victoria down the stairs." Declan shares bluntly.

My face drains of all color that I just assumed since he was an empath that Rafe was compassionate like me. He used his gift to blend in with others so they wouldn't know what he was truly like.

"Rafe is psychotic," I whisper as all the pieces come together. "I was dating a psychopath and I didn't even know it."

"When I told Nicole, she told me to just kidnap ye," Declan explains. "She came up with her idea shortly after that."

"She knew how I would feel if I gave my virginity to him and then learned later what he really was. It would be almost more than I could bear." I confess as I begin to cry once more.

James pulls me up on his lap and cradles me while I gain control of my emotions. I feel like all I have done is cry lately.

"How long have you been talking to Nicole?" I ask Declan as I cuddle into James' chest with my head right over his heart.

"She found me right after ye moved." Declan shares with me honestly. "She was determined to reunite ye with yer Declan." He chuckles.

"I will have to thank her." I smile at Declan bashfully.

"Alright," James states firmly. "Journee is still just turned sixteen years old. There will be absolutely no sex at all! I do not have a problem with the two of you being an official couple, but she will not be going to your plantation unchaperoned, ever."

"Aye, sir," Declan vows with his hand over his heart solemnly.

"You better not be bullshitting me, man," James says, his voice nearly furious. "Journee means the world to me and I will kill anyone who even contemplates hurting her."

"Then we are on the same page, Mr. Erickson," Declan replies in the same solemn tone.

"Good." James nods his head, satisfied. "If you ever just disappear again without notifying me of where you are going and when you will be home, I will ground you until you are thirty."

"Duly noted," I whisper into his chest without moving from his embrace.

"Good." He nods once again before he sets me on my feet. "Go shower and change clothes for dinner. Irish boy here can help me in the kitchen."

I scurry upstairs to my bedroom with a grin on my face. James has already given Declan a pet name which tells me that James has accepted him. James is nearly forty years old and is definitely old enough to be my father and Declan's as well. I definitely feel safe around the two of them.

When I step back into the kitchen it suddenly occurs to me that no one thought to ask Declan if he knows what happened to Ansen. I know it would be rude of me to just look in his thoughts, but I am afraid of what Declan will tell me. Taking a deep breath for courage I step up to Declan with a questioning expression on my face.

"Do you know what happened to Ansen?" I ask him softly. "He disappeared around the same time that you showed up down here."

"My connections have been unable to locate him," Declan states uncomfortably.

I nod, feeling disappointment that no one seems to be able to locate my stepfather who wants to brutally rape me.

James made sirloin steaks on the grill with sautéed mushroom and onions, baked potatoes, dinner salad, and garlic bread. I am amazed at how much food that Declan puts away while I barely manage to eat half of mine. I shake my head at the unfairness that guys can eat like complete pigs and not gain an ounce of weight while girls have to be careful not to smell it too much.

I clean up the kitchen while James takes the opportunity to get to know Declan a little bit better. When I step back into the living room where the guys are sitting and talking, James looks up at me with a sad expression.

"I want to show you something," James says as he stands up and has me follow him into his office. On his computer is a gravestone that he has ordered for Ivan. I tear up as I see that it comes with a photograph of the beloved wolf right on the stone.

"I thought we would bury him in the middle of the garden so we can sit and visit with him whenever we want," James says, emotion clogging his throat. I nod and embrace him tightly, both of us comforting the other over the loss of our pet.

"I cannot get the code changed on our security system and Rafe has it." James changes the subject. "I have a couple extra guards coming to patrol the grounds as well as inside the house until I can get the security system updated tomorrow morning."

My stomach lurches painfully because I know Rafe would love to hurt me for sharing with everyone his most personal thoughts.

"If you will allow it, I will stand guard inside Journee's room." Declan states. "It is important that she can get some sleep and I believe with my protective presence in the room she will be able to sleep."

James looks at him thoughtfully for almost an entire minute before he finally nods his assent.

"I would be unable to guard only her bedroom," James explains. "It would leave the rest of the property vulnerable."

"Understood." Declan agrees with a serious nod.

"I would like to go see Victoria's grandmother tomorrow," I suggest softly. "I need to ask her some questions."

"She owns the Celestial Lotus." James states. "She's the psychic."

"Yes." I agree. "Rafe told me that Grams told him we name our first daughter after her. I don't think she really told him that, but I need to know for sure what she told him."

"We can bring you over there after the security system is fixed," James replies with a nod.

"I'm going to go work on some homework." I head out of the living room. "I need to take my mind off of everything."

Declan follows me up to my bedroom and looks around at everything while I get started on my computer. I work on my calculus class until my eyes are crossed and I am exhausted enough to finally fall asleep.

CIRCLE OF LIFE

Declan is still standing at the window when I open my eyes the next morning.

"Have you moved from that spot at all?" I ask after yawning, sitting up in bed, and feeling bad that he didn't get any sleep.

"Aye." He replies as he turns to look at me with a heated expression on his face. "Good morning lass. Ye slept well." He states knowingly. I blush from the look in his dark eyes as I slip from the bed and step up to him bashfully. Raising my face to his expectantly he leans down and kisses me tenderly.

"My Declan," I whisper in amazement. Never in a million years did I think at ten years old that the older boy would actually be mine.

"Aye." He murmurs huskily as he strokes my cheek softly. "James wants ye to shower and dress as soon as ye wake up lass and meet him downstairs."

I shower and dress quickly wondering what is up as Declan and I make it down to the kitchen in twenty minutes. James is chatting with the security technician when we step into the kitchen. The technician shakes hands with James before making his way to the front door.

I pour Declan and myself a mug of coffee, adding cream and sugar to mine, and then turn to James expectantly.

"I know you want to go see Nadia this morning and I would like us to lay Ivan to rest before we go," James tells me. I nod and after another sip of my coffee, we make our way out to the garden where James has already dug a hole. Ivan is wrapped in a blanket when James places him gently in the ground and covers him up with dirt. I can't stop the tears that are practically gushing down my face as I watch the wolf get buried. James packs the dirt down and places the headstone that arrived this morning on the top. James hands me a bouquet of flowers for me to lie on the grave, which I do tearfully.

"Goodbye, Ivan," I whisper emotionally. James emotionally touches the headstone before leading us away back towards the house. A small little bark gets my attention and when I look around, I realize it is too close to be coming from one of the neighbor's houses.

"Where is that coming from?" I ask the guys who look at me rather sheepishly.

"I was hoping to show ye after we returned from the psychic's shop," Declan states uncomfortably.

"Show me what?" I ask, feeling a little eager over that cute little bark that has now turned to an all-out howl and I feel my heart just break.

"When I followed ye to the park after Ivan died, I contacted a friend of mine in Russia who had found a litter of wolf pups a few weeks ago," Declan explains. "I had him ship me one of the largest males for ye."

"You did?" I ask incredulously as I gaze up at him, thinking that I am the luckiest girl in the world to have such a wonderful man in her life.

"Aye." He replies gruffly. "It wasna a good time to show ye him now right after burying Ivan."

"Please?" I beg, practically bouncing up and down I am so eager. James comes right out and laughs at the visible distress on Declan's face. Declan nods reluctantly and points towards the garage.

Squealing, I practically sprint into the garage and come to a screeching halt in front of Ivan's old pen. There in the back corner of the large pen is a small gray wolf that I can feel the terror coming off of in waves.

"Oh, the poor boy is so scared!" I exclaim sadly.

I open the door to the pen slowly after motioning for James and Declan to stay back. Kneeling down so I am smaller, right inside the door, I send the wolf pup waves of love and assurances of safety. He whines at me plaintively as he paces back and forth in his corner before finally taking a step towards me. I stay perfectly still and allow him to make his way over to me. Eventually, he makes it just a few inches from my hand and finally approaches close enough to sniff my hand. I can feel that his fear is being replaced with curiosity and still I do not move while he inspects me carefully before deciding that I won't hurt him. He boldly climbs on my lap, curls into a ball, and promptly falls asleep. My heart melts for the little creature who feels so lost and I stand up with him in my arms.

"Luka," I whisper to the little gray furball. "You will be my Luka."

"Aye." Declan says as he wipes a tear from his face trying to hide it from James and me. "Perfect."

Luka seems to think I am trustworthy and doesn't wake up as I carry him into the house. James and I decide that we will go to the pet store on the way home from Nadia's shop to get the supplies we will need for a puppy. James explains that since Luka is a wolf it would be best to feed him a combination of red meat and vegetables since that is basically their diet in the wild.

I want to buy him a crate to put in my bedroom that will be his own personal space and also help me housebreak him. I can feel Declan's pleasure at my giddiness of having the wolf pup he got for me. I miss Ivan terribly and Luka will never replace him, but I have always wanted a puppy of my own to grow up with.

I study Declan while he is deep in conversation with James and doesn't know I am looking at him so intently. He is much taller than I remember him being at sixteen and much bigger than he looked in that photograph Dimitri showed me. He must be almost six foot six inches tall with very broad shoulders and a well-muscled frame. His hair is a dark shade of auburn and his beard is the same shade instead of being brighter like some guys with red hair deal with. His lips are full, wonderfully curved, and very kissable. He is very sexy when his expression gets all heated as he looks at me sometimes and I could listen to his Irish accent forever because it gives me goosebumps.

James sets some beignets down on the table for us to eat while we drink our coffee. Declan and James sit down with me and each grabs a beignet hungrily. Declan reaches over and pets Luka's head which causes the pup to rouse from sleep and growl at him menacingly. I can't help but chuckle that Luka feels the need to protect me already. I send Luka reassurance that Declan isn't a threat, so the pup lies his head back down and goes to sleep.

My anxiety is starting to climb at the thought of what Grams will tell me when I go to see her today. I set my beignet down on my small plate as my stomach refuses anymore. Rising from the table I bring Luka outside to make sure he doesn't have to go to the bathroom before we leave. Since it is easy for me to communicate telepathically with Luka, I can express to him why I have brought him outside and he takes care of his business right away.

James and Declan are ready to leave when I step back into the house so I keep Luka cuddled in my arms as we walk out to the SUV. I sit in the back with Luka and leave the front to the guys.

Gram's shop is empty when we step in and she smiles at me affectionately as she embraces me tightly.

"I have been waiting for you, my dear." She says as she flips the sign to closed, tells the guys to wait in the store, and then takes me into the back. She pours us some tea that is waiting for us on a sideboard before looking at me expectantly.

"Did you tell Rafe that he and I would name our first daughter after you?" I come out with the one question that has been bothering me. She chuckles.

"No, and you already knew the answer to that Journee." She says in a chiding tone. "I knew Rafe wasn't for you. I have been aware of his psychosis since he was just a toddler, but his parents were not ready to accept it until you. I told him that you were destined to be with someone else, a boy you briefly crossed paths with as a young girl and my namesake would come from the two of you."

"Rafe told me that to manipulate me," I state sadly. "I just trusted that since he was an empath like me, he was a good person."

"It is not a negative quality to always see the good in others." Grams tells me with a smile. "Your Irish boy and James will be there to protect you when that goes wrong."

"I'm not wrong to trust in Declan?" I ask her anxiously, terrified that since I was wrong about Rafe I could be wrong about Declan too.

"What do you see when you examine the Irish boy's thoughts?" Grams asks me instead of answering my question.

"Compassion and a strong need to protect me," I state in frustration. "Rafe knew how to put up a wall to keep me out, what if Declan is hiding his true self from me too?"

"A wall will not keep someone as strong as you out my dear." Grams explains patiently. "You developed your empath abilities until you opened up your telepathic abilities. All you need to do is strengthen your telepathy. Practice on James and Declan; all they need to do is picture a wall in their mind to block their thoughts from you."

"I feel so alone," I confess.

"You don't belong with Rafe just because he was an empath and your Irish boy is not." Grams hits the nail on the head. "Allow your love to grow for Declan because you will not find another man who will love you as completely as your Irish boy. Contact your mother's sister Xanthia because you are not the only one who will benefit from that relationship."

"My biological father?" I ask her hesitantly. Grams sighs and pauses for several seconds before she finally says something.

"You are too old for the fairy tale ending Journee." She says in an almost scolding voice. "There are some things in this life that you must sit back and wait for. He is aware of your existence at this point, but if you pursue him before he is ready you will never get to know your sister."

"I understand," I reply sadly.

"You cannot fix everything, my dear." Grams softens her voice affectionately. "However, you do need to contact Victoria and reassure her of your friendship. I do believe the girl is afraid that because of her brother you do not want anything to do with her."

"I will." I smile at Grams.

"I know it is hard to understand, but sometimes those that we love have to move on to make room for those that will come after." She explains to me.

"I know." I agree with a sigh. "That does not make their loss any easier to bear."

"Well said Journee." Grams replies. "Now scoot."

Grams stands and gives me a loving embrace before kissing me on the cheek and escorting me to the shop in the front.

James, Declan, and I head for home and stop at a local pet store to pick up a crate for Luka as well as other things we may need for him. James puts them all in the rear of the SUV before heading home.

As soon as I think Victoria is home from school, I give her a call.

"Hey. How are you doing?" I ask, trying to keep my voice normal.

"I didn't think you would want to talk to me again." Victoria shares with me honestly.

"Of course, I do," I exclaim, allowing my voice to become slightly heated. "You're my best friend Victoria! Just because there is a problem with your brother doesn't mean that you and I have a problem. I love you girl!"

"Oh Journee, I love you too!" Victoria replies with a catch in her voice.

"I can't believe you went back to school today," I state.

"I couldn't stay home with everything going on here," Victoria explains. "Dad had to take some personal time from work to deal with Rafe and now that Heath is in jail school is safe again."

"What's happening to Rafe?" I can't stop myself from asking.

"Mom and Dad are having him evaluated in the hopes they can have him institutionalized against his will," Victoria explains. "He fooled us all. I remember he used to be really mean to me when we were little but then all of a sudden, he was the perfect child. I guess we just all hoped he had been fixed somehow."

"Declan got me a wolf pup," I tell her, hoping to cheer her up. "You need to come over and meet him. I named him Luka."

"Awww!" Victoria gushes excitedly. "What color is he? How old do you think he is?"

"I think he is about eight weeks old and he is gray." I share with her, just as excited. "He's already pretty big. He is probably already about twenty-five pounds and his feet are huge."

"He must be so scared! Where did Declan find him?" She questions curiously.

"He was terrified when I first saw him in the garage this morning. I reassured him and waited for him to walk up to me himself. I wanted to gain his trust. Declan has a friend in Russia who found a whole litter where the mom was dead. I guess Luka has accepted me as a surrogate mom. He has been sleeping in my arms for the last few hours. He was so exhausted." I fill her in.

"So, what's the story with Declan, or Quinn or whatever his name is." She asks me, completely dumbfounded. I explain to her the whole story, starting when I was ten and ending with last night.

"Oh, that's so romantic!" Victoria just gushes dramatically. "I can't wait to meet your Declan."

"I'm really going to regret the moment I did that so many years ago," I exclaim with a laugh. "Announcing that he was my Declan will haunt me forever."

"I hope so." She firmly agrees.

"I want you to see if you can come and stay with me over Christmas break. My friend from Seattle, Nicole, is coming down to stay." I invite Victoria.

"Awesome! Count me in!" She instantly replies.

A NEW DISCOURSE

Declan has gone back to his home out on River Road now that James doesn't need the extra help in guarding me so he can get some much-needed sleep.

I walk into the kitchen where James is getting dinner ready for the two of us when I get a text from my aunt Xanthia.

'I have no plans for tomorrow night and wanted to know if we could get together for dinner?'

'I would love to have you come here and have dinner with my guardian James and me?' I message back to her, after asking James if it is alright.

'That sounds perfect. I can't wait.' She replies. I text her our address and send along an emoticon.

"I would like your help with something," I state as I watch James moving around the kitchen quickly.

"What's that?" He asks as he continues preparing dinner.

"I need you to try and block me from reading your thoughts. Picture a wall in your head that I cannot breach." I explain. "I need to practice breaking through and accessing someone's thoughts."

"Ok. Let's give it a try." He nods and I can see the look of concentration on his face as he attempts to block my access to his thoughts.

When I gently try to see what he is thinking I do indeed run into a wall and since James has such a strong mind it takes me a while to figure out how to break through it. When I succeed James just throws up another one for me to practice on and by the time dinner is done, I will need to take a pain pill for my headache.

"I think you have that figured out," James says as he passes me the pulled pork. "Gave yourself a headache, didn't you?" I nod as that small motion causes excruciating pain.

As I place food on my plate, I keep my eyes focused on my plate as I attempt an experiment.

'Can you hear me, James?' I try to communicate with him telepathically.

"Journee?" James asks, making me look up at him questioningly. He is looking at me quizzically. "Was that you in my head just now?"

'Yes!' I exclaim in his head happily. *'I want you to think something back to me. Instead of saying it out loud just talk to me inside your head.'*

'Is this something else you are supposed to practice?' James thinks to himself. I smile at him because I heard every word.

"After dinner, I want to try and do it from another part of the house just to make sure that distance isn't an issue," I suggest to him excitedly.

"How about you just try doing it with Nicole in Seattle," James suggests. "She is aware of your abilities and that is the perfect test because she is all the way across the country."

I nod as I wonder why I didn't think of that first.

'Nicole? It's Journee. Can you hear me? If you can just think something back to me.' I concentrate on picturing her in my head as I think my message to her.

I shake my head in disappointment when I don't hear anything back from her.

"I'm sure it will just take practice," James reassures me. "Kind of like lifting weights to strengthen your muscles."

Happy, my appetite is raging, and I take a little bit more of the mashed potatoes, gravy, and green bean casserole before I help myself to a buttermilk biscuit. James raises his eyebrow at me as he watches me fill my plate.

"Are you going to be able to eat all of that?" He asks in amusement.

"I'm starving and I am going to give it my all," I respond with an eager smile.

Luka chooses that moment to come up to me and I can feel his need to go outside to go to the bathroom.

"I will be right back," I explain to James. "Luka needs to go outside."

"Did he just tell you that?" James questions me disbelievingly.

"No, not like you are thinking," I tell him with a chuckle. "It's more I can just feel what he is feeling. I tried to teach him by thinking to him that he needs to go to the bathroom outside and apparently it seems to be working."

I get up and reluctantly leave my plate untouched while I step out the back door into the yard so Luka can relieve himself. He races around the yard and urinates on at least ten different things before he rushes back up to me happily. I chuckle to myself at the thought that if any of our neighbors have dogs, they are going to freak out over the new wolf smell coming from our yard.

Luka goes right back over to his bed in the corner of the kitchen while I sit back down to enjoy my dinner. After completely stuffing myself I take ibuprofen for my headache and decide to go upstairs and draw myself a hot bath.

James refuses to let me help clean up the kitchen so I skip up the stairs with Luka hot on my heels. When my bath is ready, I naturally assume that Luka will probably want to wait for me in my bedroom, but he insists on following me into the bathroom. He lies on the floor right by the bathtub after I have slipped into my steaming bubble bath.

I smile because of Luka's strange behavior, but at the same time, I feel so protected because the pup will not leave my side. I soak until the water cools, wash and get out. I French braid my hair after lathering a leave-in conditioner all over it with the intent of rinsing it out in the morning.

I look at the time and see that it is still early enough for me to do some schoolwork so I log into my computer. Luka lies by my chair while I study and after I am done for the night, I turn off the computer and take Luka outside one more time.

My headache has eased somewhat but with all of the homework I just did it is not gone completely. As I breathe in the cool night air, I still cannot believe the temperature difference between Louisiana and Washington state. It is the beginning of December and it should be freezing cold but instead, it is just a bit on the cool side.

'Are you alright out there' James' voice brushes through my mind. I chuckle to myself that I don't have to be focused on someone for them to telepathically communicate with me.

'Yes, just enjoying the cool air out here a little bit. It feels good and helps my headache.' I send back to James telepathically. *'Luka is peeing on everything again.'*

'He adjusted quickly. It took Ivan weeks before he was that comfortable.' James reminisces.

'My being able to communicate with Luka the way he understands really helps. He really missed his siblings.' I share with James.

Finally, Luka is done marking his territory excitedly and follows me back into the house. After changing into a nightgown, I climb into bed and am surprised when Luka jumps right up next to me. He makes himself at home and lies down at the foot of the bed with a sigh of contentment.

I spend a little while petting him affectionately and scratching him behind the ears before I turn in for the night.

The next morning, I am up early and working on homework right away. I feel like I have gotten away from my homeschooling a bit and even though I will be graduated from high school much earlier I still don't want to slack.

Now that I am down to only five required classes to graduate, I am anxious to choose a degree to work towards, but I am really not sure what I am interested in. I want to use my gift to benefit society somehow, I am just not sure in what area. I will have to ask Aunt Xanthia what she is going to college for.

There is another benefit to homeschooling; once I am close to completing high school, I can start taking college courses at home through the same program. I will get college credit for these classes and it gives me a jump start.

After a couple hours of intense study, I head down to the kitchen to grab myself some much-needed coffee before taking Luka outside. James does a double-take when he sees me walk in so early in the morning.

"What gets you up so early this morning?" James asks. "Did Luka wake you up?"

"No, I have been doing homework for the last of couple hours," I state on a yawn. "I have been slacking a little bit and need to try and get done with high school so I can move on to college classes."

"Aren't we motivated?" James approves with a nod. "Declan is coming over and wants to discuss something with us. He should be here shortly if you wanted to get dressed." James looks at my nightgown pointedly.

"After I take Luka outside." I agree. "He's getting a little anxious to mark his territory again."

Luka seems to hover around several spots by the fence and even when I try to encourage him to come back to me, he seems intent on the scent he has found. When I look inside his thoughts, I find that the scent has him upset. It doesn't belong here, and he wants to remember it.

Finally, he leaves the scent behind and marks his territory rather quickly. Before he will follow me back inside the house he stands at attention and looks around carefully, like he is looking for something.

"I thought you were going to change clothes before Irish boy got here?" James states when I walk back into the kitchen to refill my coffee.

"Luka smelled something he didn't like by the fence in several spots. I couldn't get him to leave it alone. He refused to mark his territory before he smelled it enough to remember it." I explain with a shrug as I smile up at Declan happily.

"Good morn lass." Declan greets me in his husky Irish accent. He steps up to me and ignores James' warning growl to give me a chaste kiss on the lips. I lean into Declan's arms and lie my head on his chest for just a few seconds.

"Good morning," I murmur into his chest before reluctantly leaving the kitchen for my bedroom, Luka permanently at my heels.

I shower, dress, and am back in the kitchen in fifteen minutes with a nod of approval from James.

I step up to Declan and have him kneel down with me in front of Luka. I send the pup a mental image of Declan as my mate so that Luka will accept him as his alpha and part of the pack. Luka taps his nose underneath Declan's chin before rolling over onto his back and showing his neck.

"What did ye just do?" Declan asks me curiously.

"I told him that you are my mate and as such you are his alpha as well as being a part of his pack," I explain. "Come here James."

James has his eyebrow raised when I look up at him standing there watching me.

"Mate?" He asks incredulously.

"Luka is not going to understand something as human as a boyfriend." I point out logically. "It is important that Luka understands who will help him protect me."

James comes and kneels next to us so I can share with Luka mentally who James is in the pack. Luka accepts James as another alpha of the pack that he must submit to as well as trust him to protect me.

Once I have that out of the way, I wash my hands before I sit down at the table and grab a beignet off the plate to go with my fresh cup of coffee. Declan sits down next to me and pops a whole beignet into his mouth with a moan of pleasure.

"I am going to open a shelter that specializes in women and girls." Declan states. "I have already found a piece of property that will suit my needs. I am not too familiar with New Orleans and will need to hire some reliable people to run it, provide counseling, find runaways and that sort of thing."

"I may know a couple people who can help you out with that," James says thoughtfully. "When we introduce you to Victoria's father, Dimitri, he may know someone as well since he is in the FBI."

"There are a few girls from the Seattle area that I helped to go home after being prisoners in the organization for so long and they are willing to take classes to work there," Declan explains. "They will be excellent with helping out the runaways."

"Why are you doing this?" I ask him curiously, wondering what happened in his life to want to give back so much.

"My mum was abducted from her family and forced to stay with my father, who was then head of the Incorporated in Ireland. She was killed for trying to help a young girl escape, as an example to the other girls." Declan explains. "I was thirteen when she died. I promised when I became head of the organization, I would do what I could to help, in her honor."

"I'm so sorry." I express sincerely. "No wonder you wanted to punish Ansen for what he did to my mother."

"Aye." He nods gravely. "I was hoping ye would help out at the center under certain circumstances with yer gift."

"I would love to." I nod with a smile. "I can't wait to see it."

"I am having a construction crew giving me an estimate at the moment so it will be a while before it is ready to be seen," Declan says with a smile.

"I would like to take Luka to the park today so he can get some running in and I can socialize him a little," I suggest to James hopefully.

"As long as it is early," James replies. "Your aunt is coming to dinner and I will need time to prepare it."

"I can take Journee and Luka to the park." Declan states. "I doona have anything going on today."

James looks at us thoughtfully as if he doesn't trust Declan to be alone with me at a public park.

"Seriously?" I say sarcastically. "Declan and I are going to get it on behind the first big tree we come upon."

"He is a grown man!" James thunders. "Grown men have appetites that are not suitable for teenagers!"

"He is also determined to not hurt me so that should ease your worries." I point out logically.

"Journee, it is my job to protect you." James insists.

"And you are doing a wonderful job," I reassure him. "Declan? Do you have any intentions of taking my virginity any time soon?"

"Och, lass!" Declan exclaims, angry for being put on the spot. "Nay. Ye are entitled to grow up first."

"See?" I exclaim. "I'm glad that you are worried about me, but it is alright for you to trust us too."

"Duly noted," James growls as he glares at Declan. Declan raises his hands in surrender.

"What are we having for dinner tonight?" I ask curiously, anxious to change the subject.

"Chicken and shrimp alfredo with all of the fixings," James informs me, his voice a tiny bit more relaxed. "Make sure you bring Luka's harness and leash just in case you need it."

OBSTRUCTION

Declan and I go to the large park that the Audubon Zoo is in and take Luka to the opposite side where there is a wooded area. As we walk through the woods with the pup, I let him off of his leash so he can run as I keep tabs on him mentally.

Declan gets an unexpected phone call and I walk ahead with Luka to give him some privacy. After a few minutes, I hear Luka barking furiously at something, so I run ahead quickly to see what is wrong and slip on the edge of a hill. I tumble down the hill and have the wind knocked out of me as I slam into a tree at the bottom. Luka stops barking and is at my side instantly sniffing me to see if I am alright.

"I'm ok," I whisper to him as I reassure him mentally as well.

"Are you ok?" I hear a familiar voice state and when I look up, I see Rafe sneering down at me excitedly. His desire to brutally hurt me just comes off of him in waves.

Luka sniffs at him and instantly takes a defensive pose before growling at him low in his throat. When I peek into Luka's mind, I can see that Rafe is who he smelled by the fence, just like I suspected.

'Declan.' I reach out telepathically but feel like it bounces off of something, almost like I am inside a bubble.

Rafe's smile turns to a leer.

"No one can hear you Journee." He says as he gazes down at me proudly.

I send an image of Declan into Luka's mind, mentally commanding him to go and get him. Luka whines, obviously not wanting to leave me with a threat, but reluctantly runs off in search of Declan.

Rafe tries to tackle the wolf pup but Luka slips out of his grasp after biting his hand savagely. Rafe kicks me in the ribs furious about the bite from my pup. I groan at the sharp stabbing pain that rips through my entire midsection and curl into a fetal position to protect myself.

Rafe continues to kick me while he yells at me in a rage over how I ruined his life and how I belong to him, not some Irish scumbag. I curl myself into as tight a ball as I can and keep my head tucked in to protect myself as much as I can while I keep up a telepathic chant to Declan and James.

'Help me, Rafe is here.'

I hear feet hitting the ground and then suddenly I am not being kicked anymore. I stay curled into a ball, too afraid to look around and see if I am rescued. The pain in my chest is so bad I can barely draw a breath let alone cry or scream.

Luka is there right after the kicking stops and he lies alongside me and whines plaintively. Within minutes there are cops everywhere and Declan is kneeling beside me.

"Journee lass, are ye alright?" He whispers into my ear, his voice hoarse from emotion.

'Hurts to breath.' I send him telepathically, not wanting to breathe enough to speak.

"Ye probably have some broken ribs," Declan explains as he kneels next to me and strokes my hair. "Does anything else hurt?"

'My back and hips. You hurt him, didn't you?' I am glad I am not asking this out loud.

"Aye lass." He confesses and I can feel his helpless rage at not being able to protect me.

I can hear someone sliding down the hill and suddenly James is there next to me which just makes Luka whine more.

"Did she call out to you?" I can hear James ask Declan.

'Declan doesn't know yet that I can communicate with you guys telepathically. Rafe was able to prevent me from reaching Declan or you. He created some sort of bubble where my transmission bounced back to me.' I send it to them both just to save myself from repeating it.

Declan looks dumbfounded for a second before I feel his anger just soar.

'The only thing I could do was to send Luka after Declan.' I explain to them both.

Paramedics finally make it down the hill and without moving me much evaluate me as they ask me many questions. When they have determined that it is safe to move me, they strap me onto a long plastic board and carry me up the hill. I attempt to reassure Luka that I am alright as well as for him to stay with James and Declan. The poor pup wants to come with me desperately and he whines and howls as I am taken away. James holds him firmly and speaks to him soothingly, but Luka will not be calmed.

Declan rides along with me and leaves the pup to James. I can feel James' frustration because he doesn't want to be apart from me, but he allows Declan to ride along instead.

'I'm going to be fine.' I share with James mentally and send him a burst of my loving reassurance.

The jarring and bumping as they carry me up the hill to the waiting ambulance is excruciatingly painful and I cannot help but scream a couple of times. I think Declan is swearing at the paramedics in Gaelic because I cannot understand a word he is shouting.

Finally, they get me into the back of the ambulance with Declan sitting next to me worrying way too much. The paramedic puts an IV in my arm and starts some pain medication right away to help make me more comfortable. I feel instantly woozy as the medication takes effect and after that things start to get a little fuzzy for me.

I vaguely remember being in the emergency room for a long time while they run tests to see what is broken. Fortunately, after the brutal beating I took from Rafe I only have three broken ribs and many bruises. The doctor explains to me that none of my internal organs are in danger from my broken ribs and that it is alright for me to go home. He gives the discharge instructions to James with all the explanations that are needed.

It is nearly dinner time when I am finally released to go home and I am gently placed into the SUV. James and Declan make sure I am lying down on the ride home. There is a strange car in the driveway and when Declan picks me up to carry me in the house, I see that Aunt Xanthia has arrived for dinner.

She steps out of the car, sees me in my hospital gown, and immediately brushes my mind with her gift.

"Journee?" She asks anxiously as she rushes over to me. "What happened?"

"I ran into an old boyfriend at the park," I explain, shame making me blush. "He broke a couple of my ribs. I will be fine in a few weeks. Please, come in. We can at least visit for a little bit."

She follows us into the house even though I can feel that James would rather I go to bed and get some rest. Declan sits in one of the oversized recliners in the living room with me cradled on his lap while Aunt Xanthia and James take the couch.

"This is my guardian James Erickson and my boyfriend Declan O'Shea." I introduce everyone. "This is my mother's sister Xanthia."

James shakes her hand and Declan nods a greeting to her politely.

"My first day of school here in New Orleans I met a guy who is also an empath," I explain to Aunt Xanthia. "I naively thought he was a good person since he had the same gift as me, but I was very wrong. Rafe and I became an item right away. I never searched his thoughts because I have always believed people deserve their privacy. Long story short, I discovered that Rafe was in fact psychotic and when I did look into his thoughts, I discovered that he likes to hurt girls. I shared this fact with other people so he couldn't do it anymore and now he wants revenge."

"What exactly did he do to you?" Aunt Xanthia asks. I look over at James for a second because I can feel Luka's anxiety. The pup knows I am home, and he wants out of his pen in the garage desperately.

"Will you go get Luka? He knows I am home." I ask James before turning back to Aunt Xanthia. "I took my new wolf pup for a run at the Audubon Park today and I got separated from Declan. I slipped and fell down a hill, knocked the wind out of myself when I struck a tree. Rafe must have followed us because he was there before I could stand up. When I tried to communicate telepathically with Declan to warn him, I was in danger it bounced back to me. Rafe somehow created some sort of a bubble so my transmission wouldn't go through."

"I have never heard of someone being able to do that." Aunt Xanthia replies pensively.

Aunt Xanthia's facial expression suddenly lights up.

"That's why you look so familiar!" She exclaims. "You are the guy from the news who disbanded the Incorporated!"

"Aye." Declan agrees, his expression reflecting his dislike of being recognized.

"I'm sorry." Aunt Xanthia apologizes, most likely feeling Declan's emotions.

"Nay, it's alright," Declan reassures her. "I should probably get used to it.

"I was going to invite you over to your grandparent's house for dinner this weekend." Aunt Xanthia states sadly. "I guess we will just have to wait."

Luka streaks into the room and I instantly scold him mentally, so he doesn't jump on me. He skids to a halt and whines plaintively because he wants to reassure himself that I am alright.

"Luka," I whisper to him gently, hold my hand down to him and watch as he scoots along his belly to me. He nuzzles my hand before he pretty much washes it thoroughly in his happiness. I send him my love into his thoughts as well as reassurance that I am fine.

He lies next to the recliner with a sigh and relaxes now that I am home safely. I look over at James afraid to ask him if it is alright if my grandparents come over for dinner this weekend.

"James?" I ask as I look away from him uncomfortably.

"I would love to have your grandparents and aunt over for dinner this weekend," James says without hesitation. "I think you will be feeling a little better by Saturday night to entertain guests if you take it easy."

I can feel Aunt Xanthia's burst of happiness at James' announcement and I am pleased that I am already so important to her.

"I wanted to ask you what you are going to college for?" I ask Aunt Xanthia.

"I want to be a surgeon." Aunt Xanthia tells me. "I should be starting my residency soon."

"I will be done with high school soon and I want to go into a career where I can use my gifts, but I am feeling unsure," I explain to her. "I don't think medicine is for me."

"There are all kinds of fields you can go into where your abilities will help you; psychiatry, law enforcement, fortune-telling, women's shelter, teacher." Aunt Xanthia lists a few. "Really, the possibilities are endless. You just have to find out where your interests lie and go from there. What are your favorite subjects in school?"

"I like science; when we do stuff in the lab with all of the machines. I don't know how my abilities will help in a lab setting though." I confess.

"You have plenty of time to figure out what you want to do." Aunt Xanthia explains to me. "There may be a class that you take once you start college that really helps you to decide. Required classes will take you at least a year or two to complete before you can really start taking the fun classes anyways."

She stands up and smiles at me affectionately.

"You are exhausted Journee." She states. "No, don't tell me that you will be fine. Your exhaustion is reaching out to me."

She steps towards me and Luka raises his head with a growl.

"It's ok," I tell Aunt Xanthia. "Step up to him with your hand out."

I communicate with Luka that Xanthia is a part of our pack and not a threat. She follows my instruction and Luka wags his tail at her acceptingly. She leans down and kisses my cheek.

"Get some rest. I will see you Saturday." Aunt Xanthia says before she sails out the door.

DECISION

The next three days pass in a blur of pain pills and sleeping. James is pretty scarce and seems to have allowed Declan to take charge of my care, which I know must drive my guardian crazy.

Declan insists that I stay awake long enough to eat and refuses to leave my side, except to take Luka outside. He has been sleeping next to me because he is afraid if he sleeps in another room, I may have nightmares. I cannot believe I have found such a wonderful man to have in my life. He treats me as if I were made of crystal and that I am the most important part of his life.

Finally, by Friday I get out of bed to make it to the couch to sit for a little while before exhaustion sends me back to bed for a while. You would think after all of the sleep I have gotten that I wouldn't get tired so easily.

"I don't think you are ready to entertain guests tomorrow." James appears in my room suddenly, Friday afternoon.

"They are my grandparents, so I don't have to entertain them," I argue with him softly. "I get to talk to them, get to know them a little bit, and eat a meal with them when I will already be eating anyway."

"We can watch to make sure she isna in pain or too tired to visit any longer." Declan points out to James as he reclines next to me on the bed.

"You're too stubborn for your own good," James tells me in frustration. I shrug nonchalantly, knowing I will get my way.

"You don't have to cook all the time you know," I state logically. "You are always spending so much time in the kitchen cooking complicated meals."

"I am having a chef friend of mine come tomorrow to cook for us so I can spend more time visiting," James explains with a smile. "I like cooking. It's relaxing."

"You know, now that you aren't a bodyguard anymore why don't you try dating?" I ask him, knowing it will make him uncomfortable as I grin mischievously. "You're attractive for an older guy."

Declan practically chokes as he tries not to roar with laughter at the look on James' face. Without another word, James turns on his heel and storms from the room.

I start to chuckle and the pain in my ribs instantly sobers me.

"I will have to remember to tease him when laughing doesn't hurt," I state sadly.

"That was grand!" Declan wipes the tears from his eyes. "He was truly frightened."

"Why would that frighten him?" I ask Declan confused as I cuddle up to him. "You are happy with me in your life. Why wouldn't James want the same thing for himself?"

"James has been a bachelor his entire life lass," Declan explains. "Being yer guardian is a huge enough change. It isna easy for him to raise a sixteen-year-old lass, let alone add dating a woman as well. There is a lot of compromises when ye are in a relationship and he hasna had any of that."

I nod even though I still don't understand why it would scare him. I would think that a man as attractive as James would want to be intimate.

Declan runs me a bath so I can soak because the last few days all I have had is a sponge bath, so I feel gross. I am a little uncomfortable because Declan will have to see me naked to help me into the tub without hurting myself. I still don't have a very good range of motion and I don't want to slip and hurt myself.

He helps me into the bathroom and lifts my nightgown off while I keep my gaze focused on my toes as I blush a bright crimson. I am afraid if I look up and see that heated expression in those dark eyes of his I will want to kiss him. We truly shouldn't do that while I am completely undressed. I have not been wearing any panties because it is easier for me to use the bathroom pain-free. Declan holds my arm tightly as I step into the hot water and sit down slowly with a sigh of pleasure as the steaming water surrounds me.

Finally, while I am covered in bubbles I look up at Declan and see that my nakedness did affect him. He leans down slowly and kisses me so tenderly it brings tears to my eyes.

"I am the luckiest girl in the world," I whisper to him emotionally.

"Nay lass, I am the lucky one." Declan murmurs, his Irish brogue thickening. "Call me if ye need me."

He steps back into the bedroom leaving the door cracked and I hear the bed creak slightly as he sits down. Luka positions himself next to the tub with a sigh as I lie back and enjoy the hot water. The warm water helps my ribs to feel a little better and I soak until it cools before washing.

"Declan? Can you help me out?" I call hesitantly. He steps into the bathroom after I have started draining out the water. He holds a large towel over one arm while he lets me pull myself up with his other arm. Using his arm as support I gingerly step out of the tub being careful to not step on the pup and lift my arms while Declan wraps me in a towel. He helps me wrap my hair in another towel before I walk into the bedroom to sit on my loveseat.

This is the best I have felt since the assault as I relax on the loveseat with a contented sigh. Declan comes to sit next to me and strokes my cheek affectionately.

"It's grand to see ye feeling better." His husky accent brushes over me. I lean over against him and he pulls me into his arms with a sigh.

"It's nice to not be in a drug-induced coma," I reply as I cuddle into him happily. "I love that you have never left my side this entire time," I confess to him, not wanting him to think that I take him for granted.

"I wouldna leave ye alone at a time like this lass." He squeezes me affectionately. "Are ye nervous about meeting yer mum's parents tomorrow?"

"I am, very much," I tell him. "My mom ran away from them and I am sure she thought she had a good reason. I think what scares me most is that they will try to be controlling with me too?"

"Your aunt Xanthia seems to not have the same issues yer mum did. She doesna suffer from an arranged marriage." Declan points out. "Mayhap, they learned from their mistakes. Ye desperately want a family. Be careful of yer expectations, Journee."

"I know it." I sigh. "It is still hard for me knowing Ansen isn't my real father and it really makes me feel like an orphan."

"Ye will always have me and James." He tells me. "Sometimes family that is not related by blood is stronger."

"Maybe I will check on my schoolwork for a few minutes since I feel alright sitting up." I walk over to my desk and log into my computer to check my email. To my surprise, I see one in my inbox from my biological father, Edward Beauvais. I just stare at it for a few minutes, too afraid to open it for fear of rejection.

"Read it, lass," Declan declares from over my shoulder.

I double-click it and after it opens in a new tab, I see that it isn't from my biological father after all, but instead from my younger half-sister, Demi Beauvais.

Dear Journee,

My name is Demi Beauvais and I am your little sister. Dad doesn't know that I am contacting you so please don't tell him because he would be very upset with me. I have heard my grandparents talk about your mother over the years because they don't like my mom. I would love to meet you as I am an only child and always wanted a sister."

She trustingly includes her cell phone number even though we have never met, pleading with me to contact her.

"This may destroy any chance I have of having a relationship with him if I do as she asks," I state sadly. "I want to contact her but feel like I shouldn't do so against his wishes."

"Give it a few days while ye think about it," Declan suggests. "Mayhap bring it up to yer grandparents and see what they think. While you do some homework, I am going to stop out at the plantation. I won't be gone long, I promise."

"Ok." I smile up at him, grateful for his advice.

I work on my homeschooling for a couple hours before dinner while Declan is at his house. It really feels good to do something normal except to take pain pills and sleep. I can honestly say that I have missed doing homework.

A few minutes before six o'clock I carefully make my way downstairs and find that Declan has returned. He is helping James to set the table when I step into the kitchen. Whatever James has made for dinner is really making my stomach growl as the smell hits me. Luka whines and lifts his head to sniff the food better.

James places Luka's food bowl on the floor which has chopped-up venison with cooked vegetables in it. After the pup inhales his dinner James puts him outside with a bone that he can chew on.

Our dinner is a homemade chicken pot pie and it looks delicious. James refuses to allow me to help him clean up the kitchen and to my surprise agrees to let Declan do it by himself.

"I got an email from my younger half-sister," I tell James when we sit down in the living room. "She must have access to his DNA test because I emailed my dad through there. She wants to meet me and for me to keep it a secret from him, so he doesn't get angry."

"Did you get a hold of her?" James asks concerned.

"No." I shake my head. "I really think it will damage any hope of a relationship I could have with him. He could also refuse to allow me to see Demi unless we sneak around. I want the opportunity to get to know my dad and really don't want him to think negatively of me before we even get the chance to meet."

"Write Demi back and explain that," James suggests. "Then she isn't left wondering why you didn't get back to her and she will understand that she is important to you as well."

"Declan suggested to mention it to my mom's parents tomorrow and see what they think," I tell him.

"That is a good idea." James nods his head thoughtfully. "They may have a perspective on it that we don't have."

Declan and I retire to my bedroom where we lie on the bed and decide to watch a movie together. He helps me into a nightgown first and I am surprised when I see he is on the bed in only a pair of shorts.

Blushing, I step up to him and he picks me up to sit next to him. So many actions that I used to take for granted that my broken ribs leave me unable to do. Using my arms to pull myself up on my high bed is now excruciating. Dressing and undressing are also nearly impossible until I heal some more.

Declan finds a romantic comedy for us to watch, even though I know he would much rather watch an action flick. About a third of the way into the movie he leans over me and kisses me softly.

James pokes his head inside the door after a very brief knock and raises his eyebrow at us at interrupting our intimate moment.

"Perfect timing," James exclaims. "I would hate for the kiss to have gone any further. I'm headed to the store and wanted to know if you needed anything."

"I need some more shampoo and conditioner," I inform him before my voice changes mischievously. "You need to find yourself a woman so you will stop worrying about Declan taking our intimacy too far. If you didn't trust him you wouldn't have allowed him to take care of me by himself these last few days."

Declan keeps his head down and is choking as he desperately tries not to roar with laughter at the horrified expression on James' face.

"Journee Zacari Parisi!" James scolds me in a very paternal tone. I simply raise my eyebrow at him and raise my chin defiantly.

"I am a sixteen-year-old girl who has never dated before moving here to New Orleans and I am not going to allow you to forbid me from kissing my boyfriend," I argue with him petulantly. "You will just have to learn to trust. Now go to the store."

"Ansen should have spanked you more," James states, obviously irritated before he slams the door closed behind him. I smile brightly since I can't laugh without pain as Declan holds his stomach, he is laughing so hard.

"It's bloody fierce how you manage to embarrass him as you do," Declan tells me. "He isnae being thick. I'm a grown man, Journee and ye are only sixteen."

"Thick?" I ask, not quite sure exactly what he means.

"Foolish or stupid."

"You don't want us to go farther than kissing either do you?" I look up at him in surprise.

"Why can we not get to know each other first?" He brings it out logically. "Then we will want to take our intimacy to the next level because we love each other."

I nod knowing with that reasoning I really can't argue with him.

DYNASTY

My pain pills are the only reason I get any sleep Friday night, so anxious am I to meet my mother's parents.

Late Saturday morning I take a long hot bath to help ease the pain in my chest before trying to focus my attention on some homework. After several hours I really haven't gotten any schoolwork done but it has helped the time to go by a little quicker.

About an hour before dinner is to be served, I make my way downstairs to the living room to pace nervously for my grandparents and aunt to arrive. Luka whines as he feels my anxiety, so I finally just sit and try to calm myself at least for the pup's sake.

When the doorbell rings I take a deep cleansing breath and go to answer the door. Standing there is Aunt Xanthia and a very attractive older couple who look just as nervous as I feel. I invite them in with welcoming smiles as my heart races frantically with the overwhelming fear that I will be rejected.

My grandmother is tall, but I can see that my mother and I get our facial features and coloring from her. Her black hair is nearly all silver and her violet eyes are sparkling with unshed tears as she gazes at me.

My aunt Xanthia looks a lot like her father with the same shaped face. He is a very handsome man for his age with his graying hair and bright blue eyes. He looks very distinguished.

My grandmother pulls me into an emotional hug as her tears finally start to fall.

"You look just like my Sasha." She whispers brokenly.

"Irina." My grandfather scolds her tenderly. "Give the girl a moment of adjustment dear."

She releases me but I can feel that it is with great reluctance and I can feel her love and regret just pouring off of her in waves.

I gently place my hand on her cheek as my own tears start to trickle down my cheeks.

"She knew you loved her and only wanted what was best for her," I state, desperately wanting to ease her pain. "She wouldn't want you to feel such regret."

"Oh Cassius, isn't she just a dear?" My grandmother exclaims. Everyone sits down in the living room and there is an uncomfortable silence for just a few seconds until I do introductions.

"I hope Aunt Xanthia filled you in on how complicated my life has been these last few months." I begin as I flush hesitantly. "James Erickson is my legal guardian. He was hired by my stepfather to protect me when we moved here from Seattle. My stepfather had gotten himself on the wrong side of some criminals up there in Washington. Declan O'Shea is my boyfriend. He is also a self-proclaimed protector of mine."

"My name is Xanthia Dinescu and these are my parents; Irina and Cassius Dinescu." My aunt joins in.

"You took over as leader of the Incorporated after your brother Connor was killed." My grandfather Cassius states, looking at Declan shrewdly.

"Aye, sir." Declan nods his head at Cassius as my face pales, my anxiety climbing drastically.

"Dad!" Aunt Xanthia scolds him loudly.

"You didn't let me finish," Cassius states calmly. "I am proud of how you dismantled such a large crime syndicate and helped the feds return all those missing girls to their families."

"Thank you, sir." Declan nods his head again with a smile. "My mother was abducted from her home and forced to bear my brother and me. I promised her on her deathbed that I would make things right if given the chance."

"How did you come to meet my granddaughter?" Cassius continues, his tone is curious yet protective at the same time.

"Her stepfather brought her to a meeting with my brother Connor when she was ten," Declan explains with a fond smile. "The other lads were going to hurt her, and I stood up for her and even beat a few of them to a bloody pulp to defend her honor."

"So, you kept in touch?" My grandfather asks as he looks between the two of us with a fond smile.

"There is a bit of tragedy involved in this part of the story," Declan states as he looks at me for permission. I nod at him to continue and both of my grandparents and my aunt look around questioningly.

"Ansen had just found out that Journee was not his and that Sasha had lied to him. He was furious and was sharing with Connor that he was going to kill her and take his revenge on Journee when she was a little older," Declan explains. "Connor always recorded meetings and I saw it after Journee and her stepfather had left. After losing my own mother I vowed to protect Journee. Ansen poisoned Sasha not long later so I kept a close eye on Journee. My brother was killed as a result of Ansen, so he fled to New Orleans with Journee to avoid my wrath. I knew with Journee being sixteen that he would soon take his revenge and hurt her. I also found out that the boy she was dating here in school was dangerous, so I moved down here to be closer to her."

"Oh, you poor thing." Irina whispers, her emotions all over the place; grief over her daughter being murdered, shock that my stepfather was so horrible, and relief that I had Declan to look out for me.

"So, Sasha's fever she died from was a result of poisoning and not induced by a mosquito bite." Cassius states.

"That is correct," I state softly.

"Is there any way to prove that Ansen did this?" Cassius asks, holding his rage in check.

"No. I had Sasha exhumed and tested but the poison had already been processed and was no longer present in her system. There was no way to prove that he murdered her." Declan explains. "The poison he used is virtually undetectable unless you find it within hours of being administered."

"Where is Ansen now?" My grandfather demands to know, his anger getting away from him a little bit.

"He is missing," James announced with a frustrated sigh.

"Your aunt tells us that you emailed your biological father, Edward Beauvais." Irina takes over the conversation. "Have you heard back from him?"

"No, I haven't, but my younger half-sister Demi emailed me wanting to meet me," I explain to them. "She wants me to keep it a secret from him and I really want to meet her but am afraid he will be so angry he won't allow us to see each other openly."

"I think you are right, sweetheart." My grandfather says seriously. "Your father was furious when your mother ran away. He fancied himself in love with her and Sasha just didn't feel the same way about him. For him to find out that you have existed all this time and she didn't tell him is quite a blow to his pride. He will most likely come around with time."

"We are so sorry that you have had so much sadness in your life," Irina tells me with a loving smile. "I really hope now that we have found each other that we will bring another bright place to your life."

"You already have," I reply sincerely, another tear making its way down my face.

"So, there is a story they are missing." Aunt Xanthia points out. "I can feel the pain you are suffering but your grandparents haven't heard how you hurt your chest."

"The boy that Declan mentioned that I was dating when I first moved here was an empath like me." I begin my story. "I just assumed that he was a compassionate person, so I didn't bother to search his thoughts until I happened across one when he didn't know I was nearby. Another boy from our school had been raping girls and with my help had gotten caught. The boy I was dating, unknown to anyone, had been helping him rape these girls but staying unseen by them. Due to my digging around in his thoughts his parents brought him back to his psychiatrist where they had no choice but to believe that he was a psychopath with no conscience. Declan and I brought my new wolf pup Luka to Audubon Park to let him run when Declan took a phone call. I wasn't worried because I can communicate telepathically if something were to happen. The boy, Rafe, had followed me and somehow managed to block my telepathy to Declan. He kicked me brutally and all I could do was tell Luka to go get Declan."

"I think you need to be a bit more sheltered my dear," Irina tells me, her face sickly pale.

"I think I am safe for the moment," I state with a smile. "Ansen hasn't been seen and both the boys I went to school with are in either jail or a psychiatric ward."

"Have you ever heard of someone capable of blocking someone's telepathy?" Aunt Xanthia asks her parents curiously.

"No," Irina replies thoughtfully. "I suppose it is possible once you have tapped into your psychic abilities to practice with them until you achieve your goal. Sort of like Journee did when she opened up telepathy by strengthening her empath gift."

"Dinner is served." James' chef friend steps formally into the living room with a polite bow. I am stunned to see that he is even wearing a tuxedo. After we are seated, we are served the first course which is called ciorba de peste, fish soup, and is a traditional Romanian dish. It comes with a side of a yellow sauce I learn is a garlic sauce you are supposed to mix in with the soup. My grandparents appear thrilled with the choice of our first course as they take a spoonful with a smile of bliss.

Our next course is a thick pork stew called tochitura made in a wine sauce and topped with a fried egg where the yolk is still a touch runny. A side dish called mamaliga comes with stew and is basically a corn-meal mush with a dollop of sour cream on the top.

For dessert, we are served fried dough, sweetened with curd cheese, jam, and cream called papanasi. I fall in love with my first bite and guess that the calories in it are astronomical.

After all of the food is cleared away a white wine actually made in Romania is brought out and even, I get a small glass. If James was looking to impress my grandparents, I think he succeeded immensely.

"We would love you to join us for Christmas this year," Irina says, her voice anxiously hopeful. "All of you."

"We would love to," James replies with a happy smile.

"I also wanted to let you know that we never did anything with your mother's bedroom," Irina tells me. "By the time I was ready to tackle it something told me to leave it, so I did. You are welcome to come over and look through anything you like in there. I am sure there are things you would like to keep for yourself."

Tears begin to flow freely at the thought of exploring Mom's bedroom from so long ago. She ran away when she was just a couple years older than I am now. What treasures will I find?

"Thank you, Irina." I manage to get out between tears.

"Please, Journee, call me grandma." She says with an emotional catch in her voice as well. "You are welcome at our house any time and there is no need to call ahead. We want you to feel at home with us."

"Grandma," I whisper as we both get to our feet and embrace gently until our tears finally dry up.

My heart feels full as I watch my aunt and my grandparents leave. Never in a million years did I think I could have such a happy ending when I did my DNA test. They have embraced me into their life as if we had never been separated for the last sixteen years and are already freely showing me their love. I cannot wait to go over to their house and just sit in my mother's bedroom. To be able to see a part of her I never got to see when I was growing up. A part that she kept hidden from Ansen and me.

Did she keep a diary? Are her high school yearbooks still there? Did she keep notes that she wrote to friends or boyfriends?

Never in my life have I wished so much to have the ability to communicate with those who have already passed on. Fresh tears begin to course down my face as I hurry up to my bedroom to be alone with my thoughts. New grief rushes through me now that I have finally met my mom's family. I miss her so much right now.

I curl up on my bed and let the silent tears just flow unheeded down my cheeks as I try desperately not to sob because it will hurt my ribs. Declan scoops me up and cradles me in his arms while I continue to weep my grief over my mom all over again.

Declan murmurs to me in Gaelic while he strokes my back tenderly until my tears finally dry up.

"James spoke to yer grandmother already and asked if we could bring ye over there after mass tomorrow," Declan tells me. "Yer grandparents would like ye to go to their church with them, as a family."

"Which church do they attend?" I ask curiously.

"St. Louis Cathedral." He shares as he dries my tears.

"Are ye going to be alright seeing yer mum's room?" Declan asks with concern.

"I don't know," I confess honestly. "I have so many emotions running through me right now; excitement, grief, happiness, love, and anger. It's like they are running on a cycle and it's exhausting."

"Seeing yer grandmother so emotional over ye really made me wish I had been more successful in saving yer mum," Declan confesses. "I tried to save yer mum. I never told ye that I tried, but Connor wouldnae help me."

"You were a sixteen-year-old kid," I tell him sincerely. "I am sure you were limited as to what you could accomplish with no help. You have no reason to feel bad."

We cuddle together on the bed until I fall asleep.

VOYAGE TO THE PAST

Declan, James, and I walk into St. Louis Cathedral about a half-hour before mass starts so we can find my aunt and grandparents. As we are walking down the aisle Victoria and her parents step up to me, her parents feeling ashamed and wanting to apologize.

"Please, it isn't your fault," I reassure them before they can speak. "You wanted to believe the best in your child as all good parents should do."

"If we had followed the psychiatrists' suggestions years ago none of this would have happened to you." Dimitri, Victoria's father, states tightly.

"You cannot feel shame for actions that were caused outside your control." I reach up and cup his cheek affectionately. "How can I blame you for a what-if situation? I am healing just fine."

I lower my hand when I see my grandparents walk up with welcoming smiles. I introduce them to Victoria and her parents and feel Victoria's joy over my having found my mother's family. Victoria hugs me gently before going off to sit down with her parents.

Declan, James, and I follow my grandparents towards the front of the church and sit just a few pews back from the altar. Being Irish, Declan is a good Catholic boy as well. I know that James goes because of me and that makes me happy that he cares for me that much.

After mass James follows my grandparents to their old mansion in the garden district. It looks like one of the old plantations you see scattered around the south. It is the traditional white with black trim with the columns gracing the front porch. They live on a corner lot which affords them a larger yard that is beautifully landscaped.

I am surprised to see that they have servants when we step into the house a butler greets us to take our coats. We are led into what actually looks like a glass-enclosed atrium with tropical plants everywhere. The sun has warmed the room to the perfect temperature and the smell of the blooming flowers is pleasant. Declan and I sit on a loveseat together across from my grandparents while James sits down in a wingback chair next to our loveseat. A maid in the traditional black and white uniform brings out a tray of ice tea and lemonade for us to enjoy while lunch is being finished. I wonder if my mother lived like this too. It must have been quite an adjustment to live with Ansen without a full servant staff.

"So, you do not attend De La Salle anymore?" Grandma asks curiously.

"No. We thought it best under the circumstances that I just homeschool so I can finish high school ahead of schedule." I explain. "I only have five classes left before I will receive my diploma and can start taking college classes under the same program."

"Do you know what you want to major in yet?" Grandpa questions.

"No." I sigh sadly. "I want to do something where my abilities will help people but I just don't know exactly what yet."

"You have plenty of time to just take your required classes before you have to decide in a direction." Grandpa nods. "Obviously, you will want to choose a career that you enjoy as well. I hear you are working on opening a shelter." Grandpa says the latter to Declan.

"Aye. It is coming along well." Declan states. "The construction crew should be finished in a week so that puts our open date around Christmas."

"Where is your funding coming from?" Grandpa continues bluntly.

"My mum's family in Ireland were quite wealthy so I am using the inheritance for a good cause," Declan explains with a smile. "I plan on creating a charity to keep funds flowing for the shelter."

A maid comes into the room to announce that lunch has been served and leads the way into the formal dining room. As we walk through the house, I note all of the antiques that I am guessing must come from Romania.

Lunch is light with only sandwiches and a creamy chicken-style soup. After I eat, Grandma walks me upstairs and opens the door to my mother's bedroom. I hesitate before stepping in as I look at the lavender room and fight tears.

"I will be downstairs in the atrium if you have any questions, my dear," Grandma tells me in a soft voice.

I finally enter the room once she has disappeared and I stand in one spot for quite a while looking around at everything emotionally. Mom was a cheerleader judging from the pom-poms attached to the wall as well as pictures of competitions her squad was in. Along with the pom poms are posters of music groups from when she was in school; Backstreet Boys, 'N Sync, Britney Spears, Jennifer Lopez, and others I do not know.

Her bed is a queen-sized canopy bed in lavender and white with very feminine style throw pillows. It looks like I could just walk over to her pillow and it would still smell like her.

She has a white desk along one wall with a large desktop computer taking up most of the space. Along another wall is a makeup table with cosmetics scattered all over it. I step towards one of the two doors along another wall and when I open the first one, I find a walk-in closet full of clothes. The other door opens to her own bathroom with a garden tub, standup shower, and long vanity.

It feels so strange to be looking at all of her things from this part of her life that I knew nothing about. She has a bookshelf next to her desk that is full of bad boy romance novels and music CDs. She seemed to like girl singers along with the Backstreet Boys and 'N Sync.

I would be shocked if Mom didn't keep a diary, but I know her well enough to know she wouldn't just leave it where anyone else could find it. As I study the room, I don't see anywhere that would be a good hiding place. I wonder if there are any loose floorboards in the closet.

I enter the closet and step carefully all around, rocking back and forth to see if I can hear a creaking sound. I find one loud spot in the back corner of the closet underneath some shoe boxes. The carpet lifts up easily as does the loose floorboard to reveal a treasure of my mother's diaries. I take out the top journal and see that the last entry was just nine months before I was born; dated Saturday, February 3rd, 2001.

Not able to help myself I read her entry which she must have written after attending a Mardi Gras party with my real father Edward. She is really distressed, writing how she and Edward had sex after she desperately tried to tell him that she wasn't ready yet. He got so in the heat of the moment that he took her virginity while she lay under him crying for him to stop.

She describes her plans to use what little bit of money she has saved from her allowance to buy a bus ticket as far away as she can get. She writes that she will pick her destination once she reaches the bus station in the morning bringing nothing with her so no one will know she ran away.

I am crying by the time I finish reading her very last entry and set the journal down with a sad shake of my head. Knowing this, do I really want to have a relationship with my real father? Was he just a teenager in the heat of the moment? Did he intend to rape her or did he just lose himself for a moment? Does he regret what he did when he realized she ran away rather than marry him?

Poor Mom. After what Edward did to her I could see how marriage to him would seem like a prison sentence. What if he continued to do that to her after they married? Is he that way now? Not carrying what others feel as long as he gets his way?

I lift out all of the journals from under the floor and find a small duffel bag to put them in. Eager to just go home and think about the incident I learned about I hurry downstairs to the atrium where my grandparents are chatting with James and Declan.

"I would like to go home now," I state as I wipe tears from my face, I wasn't aware I had shed.

"Sweetheart?" Grandma asks concerned.

"Mom went out on a date with Edward on Saturday, Feb 3rd, 2001 to a Mardi Gras party where they had sex which she didn't want. She couldn't see marrying him after such a traumatic thing happening, so she ran away." I explain to her in a monotone. "I really need some time to put all of this into perspective."

James and Declan hurry to their feet and are at my side before I am done speaking to my grandparents. I can feel Grandmother's fear that she has lost me too so I step up to her and hug her affectionately.

"You aren't losing me," I tell her sincerely. "I just need some time to come to grips with what Mom wrote in her diary. Right now, I want nothing to do with Edward Beauvais even though I am really trying to give him the benefit of the doubt."

"Remember, your little sister Demi." Grandma reminds me with a loving smile. "She reached out to you for a reason."

"You're right." I agree, having momentarily forgotten her. "Thank you. I will at least email her back. I will see you both soon, I promise."

I hurry away from my mother's past. The past that she didn't want me to know about.

I retreat to my room asking Declan to give me some much-needed privacy. I really don't want male opinions after what I have read. Declan would never agree with what my biological father did, but I just need to be alone.

Luka refuses to leave me alone and after whining in the hallway outside my door for ten minutes I finally let him in. He jumps up on the sofa next to me and lies his head on my lap with a sigh. I stroke his ears while I think about my real father and whether or not I truly want him in my life.

After realizing that Ansen was not my real father and I learned about Edward I confess I fantasized that he would be the perfect father. To hear otherwise is a real blow to my reality. My sister pleading to not tell our father she contacted me comes to mind as well.

Would he just get upset with her or is she truly afraid of him? My very existence could prove to open up a secret he has kept for a very long time. What will his wife think if she finds out the truth? Does he do that to her?

My mind is whirling with just the one entry in my mother's diary. Maybe I should just tell James that I adopt him as my father.

I get out my cell phone and text Demi back explaining to her that I cannot meet her until our father agrees explaining that I really don't want to mess things up. My relationship with her is important and I want the opportunity to be able to spend time with her without sneaking around. I beg her to be patient and allow our father some time to grow accustomed to my existence.

She messages me right back telling me she understands my decision and agrees that she would rather not have to sneak around to see each other. I text her a couple pictures of myself, so she at least knows what I look like and am pleased when she sends me a couple.

Demi is a small girl like me with long beautiful fine medium brown hair that reaches her waist. She has an oval face with a pert nose, full curvy lips, and big brown eyes. She is an adorable girl.

I am relieved that she understands my reasons and doesn't seem hurt by my decision at all. Now that I have thought about this issue, I turn my attention to my homeschooling to do something constructive. Declan pokes his head in several hours later to check on me and let me know dinner is ready only to find me working on schoolwork.

"Come on." He has to practically drag me away from my computer. "Ye cannae skip dinner."

Reluctantly, and really with no choice in the matter, I go downstairs to the kitchen to find James has made fried chicken with mashed potatoes, milk gravy, corn on the cob, and buttermilk biscuits. The smell makes my stomach growl and I am instantly happy to have been dragged away from my computer.

Declan raises his eyebrow at me in an I told you so fashion as we sit down at the table together. I blush lightly as I dig into the mouthwatering chicken with gusto. The mashed potatoes are rich having been whipped with sour cream, the milk gravy tastes just like the chicken and the buttermilk biscuits are homemade and utter perfection.

"So, are you still wanting to meet your biological father after reading your mother's diary?" James asks bluntly.

"Don't know," I reply honestly. "I definitely want to meet my sister Demi and to do that, I will have to meet the sperm donor. I will listen to his side if he is willing to share it, but as of right now I think I am fine not having a relationship with him. In fact, I would rather adopt you and call you dad because as far as I'm concerned you have earned the title."

James and Declan's faces both reflect shock at my announcement, and I smile at James affectionately.

"I would be indeed honored if you would allow me to call you Dad," I state seriously after swallowing a mouthful of delicious chicken.

"Nothing would please me more, kiddo," James says, his voice slightly choked up.

REUNION

After spending a small amount of time in my mother's room I pass the next week and a half dedicated to my homeschooling. I spend evenings reading my mother's diaries starting from her first one when she was only eight years old. I spend a lot of time just laughing over the silly drama she wrote about regularly and love being able to get to know the side of her I never knew.

Declan spends every night with me in my bedroom, refusing to sleep at his plantation out on river road for fear I may have nightmares. I think the truth of it is that neither one of us can sleep without the other next to us anymore. James, Dad, as I now call him, is not in agreement with this and complains frequently about it, but both Declan and I just ignore him. Besides, it isn't like we are actually being intimate with each other yet.

Declan has been busy working to get his shelter open before the holidays, so he is gone from early morning until I am lying in bed waiting for him to come home.

I have settled into a routine that I enjoy without any drama or danger these last couple of weeks and I find I am enjoying my life now.

Victoria, Nicole and I conference call every night in my bedroom as they fill me in on things I am missing at school, both in Seattle and New Orleans. I am pleased that the girls seem to like each other, and I think we will all get along fantastically over Christmas break.

I have visited Nadia, Grams, at least a couple days a week just to spend time with her and stay caught up. I feel a bond with her that I only felt with my mother and I need to spend time with her often just for my sanity. Wednesday, December 20th arrives, and I wake up extra early completely excited to go pick up Nicole from the airport. Her flight doesn't land until ten o'clock, but I am showered, dressed, and down in the kitchen making a pot of coffee by six because I just can't sleep. Declan grumbles that he planned on sleeping in this morning but joins me for coffee in the kitchen anyway.

Dad gives me a look of surprise when he walks into the kitchen, wearing only a pair of pajama pants, to make coffee and finds I have beaten him to it.

"You must be excited to go pick up Nicole." He murmurs as he pours himself a large mug of black coffee. I grin at him and practically bounce up and down I am so eager.

"Yep. Get ready for all the peace and quiet to disappear because Nicole is a whirlwind most people don't know how to handle." I exclaim as I stir my cream and sugar into my coffee.

Dad only grunts as he sits next to an equally quiet Declan at the table. I join them and sip my coffee with a contented sigh as I examine Dad's looks. It is funny because there is no way people would ever believe he is my real father with his blonde Scandinavian looks compared to my black hair and obvious Romanian facial features. I may not have the darker skin tone that is common in Eastern Europe because of my purple eyes giving me porcelain skin that never burns or tans, but my paleness doesn't make me look like him either. I am about five feet tall and can only be described as dainty whereas he is at least six and a half feet tall with a largely muscled build that would intimidate most men.

I am glad that James agreed I could call him Dad because the big oaf sure has grown on me and I couldn't imagine loving my real father as much as I love him.

"What?" Dad growls as he yawns loudly.

"I'm just glad that I can call you Dad," I state simply with an affectionate smile. "My biological father will never earn the love I already feel for you."

"Thanks, kiddo," Dad replies gruffly, coloring slightly from my emotional honesty. "I couldn't have asked for a better daughter." He reaches over and ruffles my hair with a grin.

Once he has had a full mug of coffee Dad gets up and starts to whip up a batch of French toast, scrambled eggs, breakfast sausage with a fresh fruit salad of watermelon, muskmelon, strawberries, and red and green grapes.

Declan disappears upstairs to shower and dress before heading down to the shelter for the day after kissing me chastely on the cheek.

"So, what are you planning on doing while Nicole and Victoria are here?" Dad asks as he finishes up breakfast.

"I'm sure that Nicole would like it if we took her to some of the tourist attractions. There are some I have never seen either. Plus, we can see a movie or two, I can introduce her to Grams, and we can just hang out here." I state as I throw ideas out there as they occur to me.

"We could take her on a swamp tour too so she can see the gators in their natural habitat." He suggests. "Plus, there is always shopping in the quarter."

"Oh, and don't forget all of the creole and Cajun food we can have her try." I suddenly think of it. "The zoo in Audubon Park."

We sit and discuss all of the things we can do together over Christmas break as we enjoy our breakfast together. I help him clean up the kitchen and then feed Luka his venison and vegetables before taking him for a walk. My poor pup really hasn't had much for exercise since I was attacked by Rafe. It is a good thing that I can communicate with Luka mentally so that he won't hurt me by yanking on his leash.

I walk him for a couple miles and let him lift his leg anywhere he pleases which he absolutely loves. He takes in all of the new scents eagerly and never gets so excited that he doesn't follow my psychic prompting.

When I get back to the house, I put Luka in his pen in the garage before Dad and I head out to the airport so we can make it through security by the time Nicole's plane lands.

I haven't been in an airport since Ansen and I flew down from Seattle in November. It has only been seven weeks since then and my life is totally and completely different now. Back then I thought Ansen was my real father, my mom had died of a bug bite-induced fever, I was an only child, I was only an empath, and my Declan was only a boy I had met once. Now, seven weeks later; Ansen is my stepfather, he is the one who killed my mother, I have a half-sister, I am also telepathic, and my Declan wasn't only my hero when I was ten years old but continues to be so today.

A tear trickles down my cheek at the drastic turn my life has taken in such a short while.

"You ok kiddo?" Dad asks me worriedly as we stand at the gate Nicole will be entering through.

"Seven weeks ago, today Ansen and I landed here in New Orleans," I explain. "My life is not even close to being the same today as it was that morning."

"That doesn't mean it is a bad thing." He reassures me. "You have me and Declan now and we both love you very much. If you were still living with Ansen he would probably be raping you regularly or perhaps had even killed you by this point. You have many other people as a support system around you. Your mother's family are now in your life and seem to be wonderful people. Your little sister is anxious to meet you and have a close relationship with you. Nadia, another psychic like you, is in your life guiding you carefully."

He wraps his arms around me and hugs me tightly as he strokes my back comfortingly.

"Thanks, Daddy," I whisper in a voice hoarse from emotion.

"Journee!" I hear Nicole screaming my name loudly. I look up and she is hurtling herself to me with an excited grin lighting up her face.

"Nicole!" I release Dad and throw myself at my lifelong friend. Thankfully, Nicole remembers my ribs and hugs me gently.

I have always been a little jealous of Nicole with her blonde good looks. She is about five foot five inches tall with an athletic build, golden tan to go along with her golden blonde hair that goes to the middle of her back. She has bright blue eyes set in a heart-shaped face, perfectly curved lips, a straight slim nose, and thick dark eyelashes.

She chatters my ear off all the way back to the house about nothing, in particular, just being her normal self. I sit in the back seat with her and my eyes meet Dad's raised eyebrow in the rear-view mirror at his shock that Nicole hasn't stopped talking once and I just grin at him.

I let Luka out of his pen and introduce him to Nicole, who just falls in love with my wolf pup right away. He follows along behind us as I give her a tour of the large house before bringing her into the kitchen so she can have a snack after her flight.

We retreat to my room where we flop on the bed together with a happy sigh.

"So, have you and Declan done it yet?" Nicole asks me bluntly as she rolls over to give me a pointed look with her perfectly sculpted eyebrow.

"Nope. He won't." I shrug at her.

"Why not?" She exclaims loudly.

"I think part of him is afraid of my dad, James, and the other part thinks he will be taking away my childhood or something," I tell her with a grimace. "I have even tried encouraging him when we were kissing by reaching down into his shorts to grab him, but he stopped me."

"Wow, my most bashful friend Journee is taking the lead in the bedroom and is shot down." Nicole laughs gleefully. "Declan is too honorable."

"I agree." I nod seriously. "We have not gone farther than a kiss. He has seen me naked because he had to help me change clothes and bathe when I first broke my ribs, but I haven't seen him in the buff yet." I pout.

"He is super-hot for a red-headed guy." Nicole agrees sagely. "If he were my Declan, I would definitely fight to see the man naked."

"I am really surprised that Dad hasn't forced Declan to sleep somewhere else," I confess. "After these last couple weeks, I don't think I want to go back to sleeping alone."

"James actually allows that?" Nicole is stunned. I nod and blush brightly. "You have no idea what sort of package Declan has?" She asks with a mischievous grin.

"Nicole Armstrong!" I exclaim loudly. "How can you ask that?"

"Very easily actually." She admits proudly. "Have you seen an outline in shorts or a glimpse when he is in the bathroom taking a shower?"

I shake my head and blush a dark shade of crimson while my naughty friend rolls around on the bed laughing her head off.

"Just because you have a boyfriend that you love and have had sex with doesn't mean I have to." I protest bashfully.

"But you want to." She goads me mischievously. I nod without looking at her in the face. "Work harder at seducing him then," Nicole suggests seriously.

"How?" I question her feeling completely lost.

"Guys are weak when it comes to sex." She explains. "If you can get him hot enough where he knows you won't get caught and he sees how badly you want him he just might give in."

I sigh in frustration and wish I were bolder like Nicole.

"Victoria was raped by a friend of her brothers." I share with her softly. "I didn't want to tell you about it until we were together."

"OMG!" Nicole breathes. "What happened?"

"Remember the guy at school I told you was raping all the girls and getting away with it? Heath?" When Nicole nods at me gravely I continue. "It was him. He caught Victoria in the bathroom after a game."

"Didn't you say Rafe was helping Heath to rape the girls?" Nicole asks me incredulously.

"Yes." I nod sadly. "None of the girls ever saw him rape them. Poor Victoria felt so betrayed by Rafe. Now they are both in jail waiting for their trials."

"Will you have to testify against Rafe for the assault?" She asks.

"Yeah. I just wish that I could testify that he raped all of those girls too, but the only proof I have is that I can read his mind." I share with her in frustration. "I heard that Heath refuses to confirm that Rafe raped the girls too. Heath is saying it was only him. I am really hoping that Rafe goes away for attempted murder then society will be safe for a time."

"I am really glad that you didn't have sex with Rafe," Nicole tells me with a shudder. "Your guilt and shame would have most likely nearly destroyed you."

"I agree." I shiver at the thought. "I still can't believe that Quinn turned out to be my Declan from when I was ten years old. How did you put that together?"

"He approached me and was honest about who he was when he met you, and how he wanted to protect you from Ansen and then Rafe." Nicole shares with a shrug. "I couldn't believe I was actually talking to your knight in shining armor that you dreamed of for so long. I told him that too."

"Nicole!" I scold her. "Now he probably thinks I am a dork!"

"Never, he loves you too much!" She disagrees.

"Come in!" I yell at the knock on the door.

Dad pokes his head in with a smile.

"I'm starving. Let's go get some dinner somewhere. You guys have been in here yacking all day long." He says.

We both hop off of the bed with eager nods and follow him downstairs. He takes us to what looks like a fast food place that is just packed with people for the dinner hour. It is called Cajun Seafood and Dad insists they have the best-boiled seafood in town.

We wait in line to order our food and we all get the same thing; boiled shrimp, crawfish, and corn on the cob. Dad has to show us how to eat the crawfish and after we get the hang of it, I am addicted. It tastes so good! Nicole agrees wholeheartedly and finishes her entire plate before I am done. I can't finish all of mine, but Dad eagerly helps me out with that.

WHAT ARE FRIENDS FOR

Nicole and I are sprawled on the living room sofa watching a corny romance movie when Declan comes in. He steps over and kisses me lingeringly before backing up to give me a heated look.

"I missed ye today." He murmurs to me in that sexy Irish accent.

"I missed you too," I reply with a seductive smile of my own as I run my hands down the muscles of his stomach lightly. He growls softly before standing up straight so I can't reach him anymore.

"Ye made it safely, Nicole." Declan smiles at my friend affectionately.

"I did." She nods at him with a naughty grin on her face and I inwardly cringe as I wonder what will pop out of her mouth this time. "Your girlfriend wants more than just kisses. You're making her unhappy."

I flush until I am nearly purple with mortification and drop my gaze to the couch in front of me.

"Och, lass," Declan exclaims in a whisper. "Doona let James hear ye encouraging that."

"You are a grown man Irish boy, I'm sure you can figure out how to make out with your girlfriend without her father finding out." Nicole scolds him without missing a beat. "If you don't start showing her that you are hot for her she is going to start thinking that you aren't attracted to her. You truly don't want her self-esteem to suffer, do you?"

I stay silent and refuse to join in either side as I listen to their nearly one-sided conversation. Declan sits down between us and sighs heavily.

"Do ye truly feel this way Journee?" Declan asks me seriously in a quiet voice.

"Yes," I confess. "You kiss me, but it is almost always a brotherly kiss and never goes any further. I think I am the only one who wants to do more."

"Aye then, we will discuss this further between the two of us." He declares with a decisive nod and a pointed glare at Nicole which just makes her giggle.

"I'm happy to help." She declares as she turns her attention to the movie once more. "Oh, and by the way, Victoria and I will be sharing the guest room at the other end of the house."

"I will see ye when ye come to bed then," Declan tells me with a dangerous glitter in his dark eyes. My breath catches in my throat at the blatantly seductive expression on his face and I can just feel it radiating off of him. I nod shyly and break eye contact while Nicole watches us curiously.

He chuckles as he leaves us to our movie, and I can finally breathe when he is gone.

"You're very welcome," Nicole states smugly. "You can tell me all about it tomorrow morning after he leaves."

"Did it hurt?" I ask my best friend anxiously. Nicole looks at me to see if I am serious.

"You know it's not the same for everyone, right?" She questions. "I didn't really have a problem. It was like a small pinch, but I was so in the mood that I didn't care. I bled a little bit and was sore for a couple days, but I think it was worth it. You, being so dainty, might have more blood and pain and you might not. I can tell you this, the more you are enjoying it the easier it is. Don't tense up, just stay relaxed."

I nibble my lower lip as I contemplate it and have a feeling that it will be a while before Declan will take it that far anyway. As soon as the movie is done Nicole stands up and pretends to yawn with a huge stretch.

"Oh, I'm so tired after my flight." She exclaims. "I think I will turn in." She hugs me and hurries upstairs to the guest room at the far end of the hallway while I smile at her. I know she was faking it and now I am nervous to go upstairs after the look that Declan gave me earlier.

He is lying in bed with his laptop, no doubt still working on his shelter when I step into the bedroom hesitantly. I take my nightgown into the bathroom where I change clothes, brush my teeth and wash my face.

Declan has put his computer away when I enter the bedroom and is watching for me with that heated look in his eyes. I step up to the bed slowly, suddenly nervous and very shy around him. He picks me up gently and places me next to him before he turns off the lights.

My heart is pounding when he leans over me and strokes a stray hair off of my cheek as he gazes into my eyes intensely. Determined to try and help this along a little bit I run my fingers over his large biceps up to his broad shoulders and marvel at the way he feels under my fingertips. He hisses in a breath at my touch and lowers his head to claim my lips with his. He has never kissed me this way, this seductively. I cling to him as I kiss him back and I hope that my anxiety will fade enough to allow me to enjoy his touch. Our tongues tangle and parry while one of his thumbs graze my nipple making me squirm slightly. I suckle his tongue into my mouth and pull him closer to me by his lower back. Arching up into him, I moan as I wish this were more like I have seen it on television.

Declan's breathing is harsh, and I feel as well as hear his growl come from deep in his chest as he presses himself into me snugly. His mouth is devouring mine as I lift my hips to rub myself against him wishing to feel more. His lips move across my jawline to my earlobe and then down to the curve of my shoulder where he kisses me deeply making me shiver.

Moving his mouth back to mine he slows things down until he finally is just gazing down at me possessively.

"Did I hurt ye?" He asks as he still tries to catch his breath. I shake my head and blush at how far our intimacy went. "I doona want ye to think that ye doona affect me."

"I felt that," I whisper boldly. He chuckles at my honesty.

"Aye. As did I." He whispers as he kisses me tenderly. Tucking us under the covers he spoons me from behind and holds me to him closely as we fall asleep in each other's arms.

I wake up the next morning, rather late, and see, to my surprise, that Declan is still asleep. I look down at his face, relaxed, and notice how much he looks like my Declan from when we were kids when he is like this. Smiling, I lean down and kiss his forehead tenderly only to be grabbed by him suddenly and find myself gently pinned beneath his muscular body.

"Good morning lass," His husky voice gives me goosebumps.

"Good morning my love," I whisper with a smile.

"Were you watching me sleep?" He asks mischievously.

"Not really. I noticed how much you look like my childhood Declan when you sleep." I confess affectionately.

He leans down and kisses me until I arch up into him, still desperate for my heart to race or my breathing to quicken. I feel his growl rumble in his chest as he raises his head to gaze down at me seductively.

"Let's go enjoy some coffee before I have to leave for the shelter." He suggests as he strokes my cheek. I nod with a smile and we walk hand in hand down to the kitchen where Nicole is already chatting Dad's ear off. I smile at the 'help me' look he gives me when we step into the room. Feeling naughty, I ignore him and grab mugs of coffee for Declan and me before we sit down at the table.

'Thank you.' I state to Nicole telepathically. I am proud when she shows no visible reaction to my speaking directly to her thoughts.

'Last night was awesome wasn't it?' She asks and I can feel her mischievous smile behind her words.

'OMG! It was the best make-out session ever!' I share with her and find it hard not to break out in a cheesy smile.

Nicole winks at me conspiratorially.

"So, what are you cooking for breakfast Viking man?" Nicole goads my dad teasingly.

"Who said I had to cook?" Dad replies sounding serious. "I fed you guys dinner last night, I'm on strike."

Nicole falls for it; hook, line, and sinker, gaping at him in shock. When I burst into laughter, she glares at him.

"That was just mean." She states as she huffs dramatically. Dad joins in the laughter before he rises from the table.

"How does strawberry cream cheese pancakes sound?" He asks as he starts to rummage in the fridge. "With lots of whipped topping."

"Mmmm." I agree wholeheartedly as my stomach rumbles.

"I guess so," Nicole states with a shrug and then gives me an eager smile.

"I think your friend needs to go back home, kiddo," Dad states with a frustrated sigh.

"I tried to warn you," I tell him as I raise my eyebrow knowingly.

Declan leans down and kisses me right there in front of Dad, a long seductive kiss that nearly makes me moan in protest when he finally lifts his head. I can just feel the frustration emanating from Dad and I refuse to look at him.

"I have to shower and head out," Declan whispers to me. "Big day today. Love ye lass."

"I love you too." I stroke his cheek affectionately.

"Please tell me this isn't a new development and I have to ban him from the house." Dad states after Declan leaves the room.

"No new development," I tell him honestly. "If you were busy with your own girlfriend you wouldn't have to worry so much about where my relationship with Declan is going. A good-looking guy like you deserves a woman to spoil you."

"Besides, a guy like you needs to get laid," Nicole states bluntly making me choke on my mouthful of coffee. Trust Nicole to lay it out there without any qualms.

Dad's face turns a deep crimson color before he wordlessly turns his attention back to making breakfast, effectively ignoring the both of us. I smile at Nicole after cleaning up the coffee I spit on the table.

I find it so surprising that a guy like James appears to be uncomfortable around women. I wonder if he was hurt when he was younger and just avoids it for that particular reason.

After breakfast, Nicole and I retreat to my bedroom where she insists on more details of my passionate encounter with Declan. I share bits and pieces as I blush a bright pink and she just eagerly takes it all in with a smile.

Once we are showered and dressed, I take out my mom's diary I read about my conception. I hand it to Nicole, open to the last journal entry, and sit quietly while she reads it.

"Oh, Journee." She whispers once she is done. "I am so sorry. What are you going to do?"

"I don't know." I shrug helplessly. "It's because of this, partly, that I started to call James, Dad. I mean, he has more than earned the title and my biological father at this point is just a sperm donor. What if Victoria had gotten pregnant from her rape? When the child grew up would Heath make a good parent just because it was his sperm that helped make the child? Just because Edward Beauvais is my sperm donor doesn't necessarily mean he is the father I need in my life. I do, however, want my little sister Demi in my life. I just need to patiently wait until Edward acknowledges my existence so I can meet Demi in person."

"Did you ever message Demi back so she doesn't think you don't want to meet her?" Nicole asks.

"Yes. I told her honestly that I want to get to know her and that she is important to me, but that we have to wait for our father. Meeting behind his back could backfire on us and he could forbid the two of us seeing one another." I explain to her with a sad sigh.

"So, I want to meet this Grams you have been talking about," Nicole tells me firmly. "I have always wanted my fortune told."

"Let's go see if Dad has forgiven you enough to drive us over there," I suggest with a grin.

Dad is in his office doing something on his computer when we step in with matching smiles.

"What's up kiddo?" He asks as he looks up, his expression serious.

"We were wondering if you could take us over to see Grams," I state hopefully.

"Sure." He nods as he closes his laptop with a click. "We can stop somewhere for lunch while we are out."

Grams gives me a warm welcoming hug when we step into the shop and then looks appraisingly at Nicole.

"Come into the back." She tells us with a smile. "I was waiting for you both to arrive this morning."

She has a hot pot of tea waiting for us and pours us all a cup after we have sat down at her small table.

"I am proud of you." Grams tells me right away. "The decision you made about Edward was a wise one. He will be in your life, but on the outskirts and James is the one who you will depend on instead. Do not worry about Demi. Your patience will win out because she needs you just as much as you want her in your life. Your stepmother also benefits from meeting you."

I nod at her as I take a sip of my tea familiar with how Grams just offers information to me at the right time.

"You are right in your plans to move to New Orleans." Grams tells Nicole. "You are also correct that your boyfriend Justin is only a childhood sweetheart."

I can see that Nicole was expecting Grams to tell her much more, but I also get a brief feeling of intense sadness from Grams before she blocks me from seeing why.

"So, A new boyfriend just waiting for you here in New Orleans," I exclaim to cover up what I felt from Grams before Nicole notices it. "It's too bad that you have to wait a couple of years to meet Mr. Hotness."

"It's ok Nadia." Nicole states with a catch in her voice. "You can tell her the truth."

"Oh, my dear girl," Grams says as a tear trickles down her face.

"What?" I ask, feeling like the room is closing in on me.

"Nicole has a rare aggressive form of cancer, Journee." Grams tells me softly. "The doctors are surprised she has survived this long. There is nothing to be done for her."

"Nicole?" I look from Grams to her in denial as I shake my head.

"That was why it was so important for me to reunite you with your Declan," Nicole tells me as a tear slips from the corner of her eye. "I'm sorry I lied to you."

"No! I need you!" I exclaim as if that solves everything. "You can't die! You're supposed to move here and go to college with me. We are supposed to have children together and grow old together."

"Nadia Nicole." Grams whispers to Nicole with a smile.

"Who is that?" I ask, completely forgetting what Grams told me before.

"The name of your firstborn, Journee." Grams tells me and Nicole with a bittersweet smile.

"That's beautiful," Nicole states in a hoarse voice as more tears begin to flow unchecked down her cheeks.

Once she is done crying, she turns to me with a serious expression on her face.

"Promise me, Journee!" Nicole practically yells it at me. "You won't stop living because I am gone. You will remember me with happiness and know that wherever I am I am watching over you. Promise me!"

"I promise," I whisper with a nod as I wipe away my tears.

NICOLE

It takes me a little time to put my grief for Nicole in the back of my mind and live for the precious memories I yet get to make with my lifelong friend. By the time we walk back into the shop my tears have dried up and we are laughing together again.

Dad takes us to another locally owned restaurant and this time he insists we try the red beans and rice because they are supposed to be famous for it. Nicole eagerly inhales hers and I know that this visit is going to be experienced that way for her, happily.

My appetite has fled with the news of her upcoming death, but I endeavor to eat as much as I can and pretend to be enjoying myself. Nicole yawns several times while we are eating and when I suggest we go back to the house to take a nap she strangely agrees.

As soon as we get home she goes back up to her room and I can feel her exhaustion coming off of her in waves as she tries to hide it from me.

"Come on kiddo." Dad stops me from going to hide away in my room. "Let's go have a glass of iced tea and talk."

Reluctantly, I follow him into the kitchen where we sit down at the table with our ice tea and he waits patiently for me to unload my burden.

"Nicole is dying," I whisper as I keep my eyes trained on my glass, knowing if I look up at him, I am going to lose it. I can feel that he is stunned as he tries to absorb my news.

"Grams told you," Dad says. "When and from what?"

"Grams wasn't going to tell me," I confess. "Nicole told her it was ok that she tells me the truth. She is dying from a rare aggressive form of cancer that doctors can do nothing about."

"Nicole lying to you about the abduction was to reunite you with Declan. This trip is her goodbye party." Dad says thoughtfully while I nod my agreement.

"Grams told me the name of my firstborn I have with Declan." I share with him sadly. "Nadia Nicole." My voice breaks on the name as I desperately try not to cry.

Dad pulls me up onto his lap and holds me while I sob my heart out. He strokes my hair and whispers consolingly until my tears finally dry up.

"Grams will be dead before my daughter is born," I state as I hiccup from so much weeping.

"Are you sure?" Dad asks uncertainly.

"Yes," I whisper into his chest sadly. "That is why it is so important for me to name her the way I do. That is why Nicole insisted on seeing Grams today. She was using it as a way to tell me about her cancer."

"How do you know about Grams?" Dad asks curiously.

"She somehow sent me her knowledge of her upcoming death mentally while we were sitting there this morning," I explain. "She doesn't know when just that she won't be able to meet her namesake."

"I'm sorry, little one," Dad tells me sincerely. "You just can't catch a break, can you?"

"Grams did warn me that I will be going through a lot of painful situations," I state with a sigh. "Nicole doesn't want me to stop living because of her death. How do I do that?"

"She wants you to remember her with happiness and not be stuck in your grief," Dad explains and I can feel his own grief over something rushing to the surface. "Nicole is probably thrilled that you have found Victoria and that she reunited you with Declan. They don't understand that you have a hard time moving on with your life when they aren't there."

"That sounds impossible," I whisper as I fight fresh tears.

"It is for some of us." He murmurs as I feel his intense pain over a memory he is hiding.

"I'm sorry," I tell him sincerely.

"For what?"

"For whoever you lost," I explain. "I won't tease you about dating anymore. I didn't know." Dad laughs, his voice is hoarse.

"She would definitely approve of you teasing me kiddo." He shares with me honestly. "She would be ecstatic that I have you in my life."

Dad and I just sit together quietly, enjoying the closeness of the other as we are each lost in thought. After a while and with some prodding from Luka I decide to go for a walk while Nicole is resting. Luka is thrilled because he absolutely loves going for walks so he can mark his territory everywhere. It is kind of funny because when we walk past a yard where there is a dog outside, they might bark at first but ultimately run off when they smell what Luka really is.

The walk outside helps me find some peace inside myself that I find I need desperately. Nicole is suffering to spend more time with me before she goes and I know that is why she is holding on, for me. That is really selfish of me even though it isn't my decision.

There is an ambulance at the house when I return and when I rush inside, I see that Nicole is being brought outside on a stretcher looking so pale she is gray. I can feel the terrible pain she is in, and it almost makes me double over it is so intense. I step up to her and try not to cry.

"I'm sorry I didn't make it longer." Nicole manages to whisper. "I wanted to try and be here for the whole vacation."

"You are the best friend someone could ever have, ya know," I tell her sincerely, my heart in my eyes. "You did so much for me, and I never got to return the favor."

"Not everyone gets a child named after them." Nicole states with a smile. "Promise me you will be alright."

"I promise," I vow. "Your mom?"

"She is waiting for me at the hospital." She tells me. "She flew down with me."

"I will tell your mom you miss her," Nicole tells me before they close her up in the ambulance.

The overload of emotions is too much for me, I feel suddenly faint and fall to the ground. I am scooped up and when I look up to see that it is Declan who has saved me from hitting the ground. Without a word he carries me into the house where I sob fresh tears because of my friend.

Dad is already pacing in the living room when Declan carries me in and sits down on one of the recliners with me cradled in his arms. He holds me until the ache in my chest is so great that I think I will die of it. The peaceful expression on her face before they closed the ambulance doors is tearing me apart. Her parting comment that she will tell my mom that I miss her. The pain I am feeling at her loss is devastating and I haven't even technically lost her yet.

Dad presses a cup of hot tea in my hands making me sip some.

"I'm so sorry baby," Declan murmurs into my ear and I can hear his pain at the loss of Nicole. I had momentarily forgotten that he probably got close to her up in Seattle after I moved down here.

All of the happy memories I have with her hurt so badly and it all seems to be centered in my chest that physically hurts terribly. She was such a wonderful friend and I feel guilty because I feel like I didn't get to give back to her.

I have cried so much I feel like I am completely dehydrated and that just seems to make my chest hurt that much more. I don't think I will be able to cry anymore if I wanted to, the tears are gone. I sip my tea while Dad and Declan worry about me and how they are going to help me through this.

'I love you, Nicole,' I send it to my friend telepathically. *'I'm going to miss you so much.'*

'I love you too, Journee.' Nicole returns. I can feel the physical pain lacing her words as she struggles for a few seconds and then there is nothing there anymore; she is gone.

The ache inside me increases a hundredfold at my loss as I set down my tea, run outside, and scream my agony. Luka hasn't left my side and he curls himself around me protectively, not understanding why I am so distressed.

Luka whines when Declan picks me up and carries me upstairs to our bedroom. He lies on the bed with me and just holds me while I feel like I am going to break apart into a million pieces. Luka curls up on the opposite side of Declan, lying by my legs comfortingly.

The next day when I finally wake up around noon and make my way downstairs to grab a cup of coffee, I hear surprising news.

"Nicole's mum was here," Declan informs me. "She was hoping to see ye but understood that we wanted to let ye rest. She is moving down here to be close to ye. She said ye were like a daughter to her. Nicole is being interred in a mausoleum here in St. Louis Cemetery."

"Nicole will be here?" I ask, feeling a brief spark of happiness. Declan nods at me and watches my expression carefully. "Did her mother say when the funeral would be?"

"Wednesday." He tells me. "St. Louis Cathedral."

"I think it is a good idea for both you and Victoria if you still go ahead with the Christmas break get-together," Dad says as he steps into the kitchen.

"I agree." Declan states. "Nicole would be hurt to know ye canceled it."

"You are right, and Victoria needs some fun too after what has happened to her." I agree, even though all I want to do is curl up in bed and feel sorry for myself.

I so badly want to reach out to Nicole telepathically but feeling her emptiness after she died was traumatic for me. I don't want to feel that blankness again.

"I need some time alone," I state, my voice sounding strange to my own ears. "I need to come to grips with this. I am going to just go outside and sit in the garden."

Both Dad and Declan nod at me as I leave the room quietly. I sit down at one of the patio tables with Luka ever at my feet. My mind travels back to my first day of preschool when I met Nicole for the first time. I was very aware of the fact that I was an empath and that I had to hide this from all of my schoolmates as well as that I would most likely never meet someone like me at school.

This made me very bashful around the other kids, so I hung back away from everyone and just watched them play together while absorbing their emotions from across the room. Nicole was a whirlwind even then at only five years old. One of the bigger boys in our class decided he was going to pick on me and he pushed me down onto the floor. He was in the process of body-slamming me when Nicole ran across the room and tackled him before tattling to the teacher. The boy got into trouble while Nicole and I became inseparable ever since.

She was always there to protect me, especially after finding out that I was an empath. None of the other kids at school knew, but my refusal to be social with anyone other than Nicole singled me out for teasing.

Nicole was friends with everyone no matter what group they hung out with or how ostracized they were. She was always the bright shining light in whatever room she was in. Her wild craziness was so heartwarming and easy to be around that everyone who knew her was drawn to her.

Nicole only had her mother since her dad left them before she was born. She was always really close to her mom. After my mom died, I was pretty much adopted by her mom and I was at their house all the time.

When all of the girls started to hit puberty and were all excited to start shaving, I couldn't join in their fun. My combination of dark hair and purple eyes actually causes me to not grow body hair or to have my period. The hair on my head and my eyebrows are all I get. Nicole was perfect at keeping my secret and would tell the girls that I went to a spa to get waxed. They were all jealous of me then.

I start to tear up a little when I remember Nicole's reaction to my meeting Declan when we were ten. She was so excited for me, and it didn't matter that I never saw him again because he was my prince charming, and we were meant to be together. I shared with her all of the dreams and fantasies I had about him. None of the boys I knew from school could compare to my Declan, not even the older boys.

"I'm so sorry, Journee." Victoria comes out and gives me a gentle hug with tears in her eyes. She sits down at the table with me and just patiently waits for me to talk.

"I found out this morning from Grams that she was sick." I share with her, my voice sounding dead. "Nicole insisted on going to see her because she wanted to be told her future. Grams knew right away I guess but didn't want to tell me until Nicole told her it was alright."

"Nicole didn't want you to have to worry about one more thing with everything that has been happening since you moved here," Victoria says. "She got to come and spend one more night with her best friend in a new city."

"I told her I loved her and would miss her telepathically after the ambulance took her," I explain, my voice choked up suddenly. "She said she loved me back and then I just felt nothing…..she was gone."

"You felt her death from all the way over here?" Victoria asks me incredulously.

"Yeah, and I hope I never have to feel that blankness ever again," I state with a shudder. "One second I could feel her ya know. What makes Nicole, Nicole, and then it was just emptiness."

"I wish I could make this better for you somehow." She tells me.

"I'm glad you still came over I really don't need to be alone right now," I tell her sincerely. "Her funeral is on Wednesday. Her mom is moving down here to New Orleans to be close to me and she is having Nicole interred in St. Louis Cemetery."

"Oh, that's great!" Victoria agrees. "Do you know how long she knew about her cancer?"

"She found out right after I moved down here," I reply. "I can't believe she is gone already. Her mom must be completely lost without her. They were all each other had."

"Does her mom know about your gifts?" Victoria asks me curiously.

"Yeah. I didn't mean for her to find out but it sort of slipped out one day." I laugh softly. "I told her how she was feeling about something before she had a chance to say anything. She had noticed for some time that I was quite perceptive about people and just put two and two together."

"Mom and Dad managed to get a medical power of attorney over Rafe," Victoria tells me. "Rafe has been placed in River Oaks Hospital. The doctor told my parents that they believe Rafe is delusional because he believes in his psychic abilities. I guess they have him on some pretty strong medication that dulls him so much he can't use his gifts anymore."

"That sounds frightening," I state in shock. "I couldn't imagine someone taking away my gifts. I am glad that Rafe is getting help because he needs it, but I really don't wish anything bad for him."

"He is my brother and I wish him all kinds of bad," Victoria confesses angrily. "To think that he was just pretending all of these years and manipulating all of us. He could have killed you."

"He didn't," I say in compassionate tones. "I read a study about people who have no conscience, and they say it happens while they are in the womb. It has to do with an off-balance of specific hormones that essentially damages that part of the brain. They are born that way."

"So, you're basically saying that he can't help it," Victoria states sarcastically.

"He can't." I agree with a sad smile. "It is good that he has been placed in a hospital where he can get the care he needs."

THE BAYOU

Victoria and I step into the kitchen and surprise Dad and Aunt Xanthia who are standing awfully close to each other and appear to be whispering. As soon as they realize we are there, Dad jumps back like we caught him having sex or something. His face turns pink, and he stirs the Salisbury steak on the stove very devotedly.

"Hi Aunt Xanthia!" I give her a big hug and kiss her on the cheek. "What brings you over?"

"I actually had some free time since I am done with school and don't start my residency for a couple weeks so I thought we all could do something together, but James just told me about your friend Nicole." She explains. "I am so sorry."

"Thanks. I only found out that she was sick yesterday and then she was gone." I confess sadly. "I'm sure Dad would be thrilled if you stayed for dinner."

"You are always welcome to come for dinner Xanthia," Dad says smoothly. "You are part of the family after all."

"I would love to! Thanks." Aunt Xanthia smiles happily.

"Speaking of family, where is Declan?" I ask curiously.

"He got a call from the FBI about a teenage girl they found in one of his brothels in Las Vegas. They needed him for something." Dad explains. "He thought he would be back for dinner."

"We are going to be doing a swamp tour tomorrow did you want to come with us?" I invite my aunt Xanthia eagerly.

"Yes! You know, I have lived here my whole life and have never gone on one of those!" She replies with a laugh.

"I'm pretty excited to see some alligators," I confess.

Aunt Xanthia, Victoria, and I sit down at the table after Dad pours us all a glass of iced tea.

"So, I wanted to talk to you about what direction you want to go when you go to college." Aunt Xanthia says. "I know you want your gift to be an asset and I actually had an idea."

"I really do want to be able to use my gift to enhance my career I just don't know what direction I want to go in," I confess to her.

"You are a very compassionate person, and you really care about people." Aunt Xanthia tells me. "What about psychology or psychiatry with the thought of working hand in hand with Declan at his shelter. By the time you get your degree and can practice he may have a string of shelters around the country."

"I have thought about that," I confess. "I would love to help Declan with the shelters and my gifts would really enable me to see things other counselors wouldn't be able to."

"If you get into a couple classes and decide that that direction isn't for you then you can always choose another degree." Aunt Xanthia says.

Aunt Xanthia fills me in on Tulane University since that is where she went and we chat about professors, classes, and all of the other things involved on the campus. After chatting for a couple hours Dad has me set the table while he places all of the food there. I worry a little when Declan doesn't show up at our normal dinner time, but I decide to call him once we are done eating.

Victoria helps to clean up the kitchen after dinner while I step outside to call Declan. "You missed dinner," I state after we greet each other. "Is everything alright?"

"The FBI wanted a sample of my DNA for comparison in case there were any girls related to our family that was found in any of our properties," Declan explains. "It seems there is a teenage girl outside Las Vegas who is my half-sister. I never realized that my father had gotten any of the girls pregnant, so I have to fly down there to deal with this. Her mother died some years ago and she was raised by the other women in the brothel, so she doesn't have any other family besides me."

"Well, she has a home here with you and we will welcome her with open arms," I tell him sympathetically. "We can get her whatever help she may need."

"I will call you and let you know what I find out and when I should be coming home," Declan says. "I love you."

"I love you too."

After hanging up I step back into the kitchen to find Dad, Aunt Xanthia, and Victoria chatting at the table where I join them with a sigh.

"The FBI ran a girl's DNA from a brothel outside Las Vegas and it turns out that she is related to Declan. Apparently, his father must have gotten someone pregnant. He is flying down there because he is the girl's only family at this point." I share with them.

"How old is the girl?" Dad asks curiously.

"He only said she was a teenager and that she had been raised by the other women in the brothel after her mother died," I reply. "He will probably bring her home with him."

"He is very loyal to his mother's memory, and I can imagine he will be quite protective of the girl as well," Dad states matter-of-factly.

"Let's go watch movies," I tell Victoria.

'Aunt Xanthia needs time to be alone with Dad.' I share with Victoria telepathically.

Victoria grins at me as we both stand up to leave the room.

'He will be more romantic if we aren't around.' I mentally send to Aunt Xanthia, and she grins but hides it from Dad.

I see Aunt Xanthia scoot closer to Dad at the table as Victoria and I leave the room. Luka follows us upstairs to my room where both Victoria and I change into pajamas before plopping on the bed. We search through the channels until we find a movie that we both like and watch in companionable silence.

Victoria and I are both up early the next morning and excited to go on our swamp tour to see the bayou. I head down to the kitchen to make a pot of coffee and let Luka outside when I happen upon Dad and Aunt Xanthia lip-locked in the kitchen.

I blush at the passion between the two of them and try to back out of the room without being noticed but Dad sees my movement out of the corner of his eye. They break apart guiltily and to my surprise, I notice that Aunt Xanthia is wearing only a super long t-shirt.

She spent the night!

'Did you guys?' I ask her telepathically as I focus my attention on the coffee pot.

She doesn't answer my question, but I can feel her radiating happy satisfaction and that is answer enough for me.

"Sorry I busted in on you guys," I state out loud as I let the coffee brew. "Victoria and I are pretty excited about the swamp tour today."

"It's alright, kiddo," Dad murmurs as he starts rummaging in the fridge to decide what to make for breakfast.

I go let Luka in the house and rush back upstairs to my bedroom where Victoria has just gotten out of the shower.

"Guess what I just walked into down in the kitchen?" I ask Victoria eagerly.

"What?" She asks curiously at my expression.

"Dad and Aunt Xanthia in a passionate lip-lock in the kitchen," I tell her with a gleam in my eyes. "Aunt Xanthia was only wearing one of Dad's t-shirts."

"She spent the night?" Victoria's eyes pop open incredulously.

"Yep and Aunt Xanthia looks extremely happy." I nod mischievously. "It's about time Dad gets some and they looked so good together!"

"I think you will be seeing a lot more of your aunt." Victoria quips with a laugh.

"That's awesome! I really hope it works out between them. Dad really needs some happiness in his life." I state hopefully.

I go take a shower while Victoria gets dressed and does her hair. She and I are ready to go down for breakfast about an hour later and once again Dad and Aunt Xanthia are kissing.

I clear my throat and they break apart slower this time after giving each other heated looks.

Dad has made turkey, asparagus, mushroom, and swiss cheese omelets with buttermilk biscuits. We all sit down together at the table and chat while we eat. Victoria and I clean up the kitchen while Dad and Aunt Xanthia go upstairs to shower and dress.

We pull into the parking lot where the swamp tours are and are fortunate that we have an unseasonably warm day for the end of December. There is no one else waiting for a tour so it is only the four of us on the boat except for the guide.

As an empath I have always loved nature for the peace it gives me, and the bayou is no different. I am surprised at how green everything is even though it is winter here. The smell takes a little getting used to but the beauty here more than makes up for it. Our boat travels slowly through the thick greenery and I get to see my first alligator after about ten minutes. I am stunned at how much bigger they are in person as opposed to seeing them on television.

I close my eyes and just enjoy the sounds of nature as the boat slowly moves through the swamp. It is like having my batteries recharged after being overwhelmed by everyone's emotions constantly. Even though I can block them for the most part it is exhausting to always have that wall up. For me to be able to just completely relax and let go is a real treat.

After a while, I open my eyes again and notice that there is a very large alligator right next to the boat. Mentally I connect with it and am surprised to feel that it is actually very relaxed. I expected it to feel aggressive or something, but it seems to be used to the boat in its territory.

My mind turns to Nicole, and I really wish she could have experienced this with me. I am glad that she isn't suffering anymore, but I miss her so much it still hurts terribly. She would have been so excited by the alligators and would have been surprised by how big they really are too.

I know that she didn't tell me about her cancer because she thought I had too much to worry about already but had I known I would have spent more time with her. It is still hard for me to believe that she is gone. I keep expecting my phone to ring with her being on the other end. Some thought crosses my mind that I want to share with her only to realize that I can't anymore.

Dad and Aunt Xanthia are whispering amongst themselves quietly and look very much like a couple in love. Victoria looks more at peace than I have seen her since Heath hurt her.

"How is your therapy going?" I ask her curiously.

"It really helps." She confesses. "I think the hardest part is learning that my own brother was helping him hurt all the other girls. Most of my nightmares have to do with Rafe and not Heath."

"Have you tried a diary?" I ask. "That is a form of venting too and helps to not keep it bottled up between sessions."

"My therapist recommended that I do that, and I just haven't." She tells me. "I have just been procrastinating. I guess it is worth it if it prevents some of the nightmares."

"Nightmares can be total torture," I tell her sympathetically. "Have you heard when the trial is supposed to start? Have any of the girls said they remember seeing Rafe with Heath?"

"It is scheduled to start at the end of January," Victoria explains. "I guess some other girls have come forward that he raped from other schools. Some of them he managed to rape at parties, others he even got away with at away games."

"Do you know how many girls there are?" I ask incredulously.

"The last count I heard was close to thirty," Victoria replies.

"After learning about all of this his parents still want the charges dropped against him so he can still go to college," I exclaim angrily. "Like colleges need more criminals on campus."

"I think he is going to go away for a very long time," Victoria says thoughtfully.

THE GYPSY CLUB

We are in the car on the way back home after the swamp tour when my email notification goes off on my phone and I am stunned to see an email from my biological father, Edward. He wants to meet with me so he can tell me his side of what happened so long ago. I just stare at my phone in shock that he actually contacted me.

I email him back that I am available to meet him for coffee somewhere. He sends me a message right back that I can meet him at his jazz club in the French Quarter *The Gypsy Club*. He will be there all afternoon if I am available today.

"Dad?" I ask hesitantly.

"Yeah, kiddo?" He responds as he drives.

"Edward just emailed me and wants to meet. Apparently, he owns *The Gypsy Club* in the quarter and says he will be there all afternoon if I want to stop by." I explain hesitantly, still rather stunned at his sudden contact.

"Do you want to meet him?" Dad asks curiously.

"I might as well get it over with." I shrug. "This way maybe Demi and I can develop a relationship."

"Are you sure this is a good idea right now?" Dad asks with concern. "You just lost your best friend, and you have no idea what this man is going to say to explain what happened between him and your mother all those years ago."

"Putting it off isn't a good idea either," I explain.

"Alright." Dad agrees. "I would be more comfortable if we all went along. Since we are already on the way there."

"Sounds good to me," I state as my stomach tightens anxiously. The drive to the club only takes another twenty minutes and too soon I am standing on the sidewalk outside. Aunt Xanthia takes my hand in hers supportively and walks me inside while Dad and Victoria follow along behind.

The interior is rather dim, and it takes my eyes a few seconds to adjust before I can make out anything. I hear a loud gasp somewhere ahead of me and when I can finally see a man is standing at the bar staring at me like he just saw a ghost.

He is a couple inches under six feet tall with a slim athletic build and medium brown hair that is parted on the side and combed back. He has a rectangular face with a wide forehead, hooded brow, patrician nose, and thin lips.

Guilt and grief are radiating off of him in waves as he gazes at me emotionally. Dad, Aunt Xanthia, and Victoria go over to a corner booth to sit down and leave me alone with my biological father. The club is apparently closed because there is no one here but us.

"You must be Edward Beauvais." I step up to the bar and hold out my hand politely. "I'm Journee."

He shakes my hand firmly and smiles down at me sincerely.

"Let's go sit down." He motions towards a table on the other side of the club. "Can I pour you a cup of hot tea?" I nod at him as we step over to the table and sit down.

We sip our tea for a couple minutes in silence as I force myself to stay out of his thoughts for the moment.

"You look exactly like I remember your mother looking the last time I saw her," Edward states with a catch in his voice.

"Yes. Everyone that knew her says that." I smile politely. "Mom wrote about the Mardi Gras party you both attended the night before she ran away in her diary," I state bluntly, done with the chit-chat. His face pales at my forward statement before he clears his throat and nods his head.

"Yes, we had only been engaged for a month when we went to that party." He explains. "Our families had always run in the same circles, so we grew up knowing each other, but not really being friends. I admit I really had a crush on her. I know she didn't want to marry me, but she went along with it to please her parents. Anyway, she and I had a couple of mixed drinks at the party. She said she didn't really like the taste, so she gave me her third drink and I drank it only to find out later it had been spiked with a date rape drug. We ended up in a bedroom and were just kissing. I remember the kissing and brief flashes of us going all the way. I don't remember her reaction to what happened at the time. My older brother knew something was wrong when I went home, and he brought me into the emergency room to find out I had a date rape drug in my system. By the time I was sober enough to tell your mom what had happened she was already gone."

I search his thoughts and see that he is being honest with me as well as the fact that he still feels terrible for what happened. I can see how Mom misunderstood what happened and was traumatized.

"Mom thought you had forced yourself on her and knew she couldn't marry you after that," I explain to him sadly. "She didn't know about the fact that there was a date rape drug in her drink that you ended up ingesting. She didn't know she had gotten pregnant until after she had met and married my stepfather." I reach across the table and squeeze his hand reassuringly.

"Is your mom here in New Orleans with you?" He asks eagerly. A tear falls from the corner of my eye and trickles down my face as I shake my head.

"She died from a fever when I was ten." I share with him.

"I'm so sorry, Journee." He says sincerely. "So, is that your stepfather?" He nods his head towards James across the club. I shake my head with a sigh.

"My stepfather didn't know I wasn't really his daughter for a long time and when he found out he was so angry he is the reason why Mom died," I whisper shamefully. "He moved us down here in November to try and get away from the Irish mob he had gotten himself involved in. Long story short, my stepfather is missing and that man over there is the bodyguard he hired to protect me who is now my legal guardian."

Edward's eyes practically bulge out of his head at my statement, and I can tell he is struggling to take it all in.

"Your stepfather murdered your mom?" Edward breathes. I nod and wipe away another tear.

"My life these last few months have been a mess," I confess.

"Have you met Sasha's family yet?" Edward questions me hopefully. I nod with a happy smile.

"Yes. I found my aunt Xanthia on that DNA sight too and have since met my grandparents. We are having Christmas together this year." I share with him, grateful to be able to share the good news.

"Are you happy living with your bodyguard?" Edward asks me seriously. "I would be happy to have you come and live with us."

"Thank you, but James is wonderful." I smile brightly at his invitation. "My grandparents tell me that I have a half-sister."

"Yes, her name is Demi, and she is thirteen years old." Edward shares with a fond smile. "She already knows about you and has been very excited to meet you. She told me that she emailed you but that you thought it wise to wait for my permission. I appreciate you giving me the time I needed to come to grips with this."

"Of course." I smile. "I wanted the chance for my relationships with you and my sister to start on the right foot."

"I would like to meet your guardian if you don't mind," Edward suggests. I nod and we walk over to the table where they are sitting.

"Edward; this is my guardian James Erickson, my aunt Xanthia, and my friend Victoria." I introduce everyone. James and Edward shake hands while Aunt Xanthia and Victoria smile at Edward.

"You are Sasha's sister." Edward smiles at Xanthia.

"Yes." Aunt Xanthia smiles at him politely. "It's nice to see you again, Edward."

Edward and I join them at their table, and I listen while James fills in my biological father on all the details of what has happened to me in the last few months. Edward seems to want to jump right into the father role with me which makes me grateful that I live with James instead. I really hope that Edward doesn't get the thought into his head that he needs to sue for custody of me because that will truly ruin our relationship.

I really hate invading people's privacy by poking around in their thoughts, but I really need to know what Edward is thinking as far as his role in my life. I am disappointed to see that he is already contemplating contacting his attorney after I leave to see what his chances are.

I stand up so fast that my chair falls over and bumps the wall rather loudly.

"If you want any chance of a relationship with me you will stop that thought right now, Edward," I exclaim furiously with my hands braced on the table as I glare into his dark green eyes. "I have had enough trauma in my life lately without you suddenly thinking you can parent me better than James."

Edward's face pales as he gazes up at me in shock.

"How did you know…" He stutters nervously as he shakes his head in disbelief. "I'm sorry. I only wanted to help you and thought if I had custody of you then you would be happier."

"You might be my father biologically, but I decide how much we see each other and if that is an arrangement that you cannot live with then our relationship ends before it begins," I state in icy tones.

"Agreed," Edward reassures me. "Demi is looking forward to meeting you and I thought she could go spend a few days with you over Christmas break."

"I would love that. I have a funeral to attend on Wednesday so if she would like she can come to stay Thursday through Sunday." I suggest in a calmer voice.

Edward and I exchange phone numbers and home addresses before I lead everyone out of the club.

"That was a little harsh, wasn't it?" Dad asks me once we get into the car.

"He was going to contact his attorney as soon as we left to start a custody hearing!" I exclaim furiously. "I am not allowing him to take me away from you."

"Understood." Dad nods.

When we get back home, I see that Declan's car is in the driveway and I hurry in excitedly with Victoria rushing behind me. Declan is in the living room with a red-haired girl that is a few inches taller than me. They are standing by the window chatting when I step into the room.

Her hair is naturally curly and falls to the middle of her back with various shades of red. She has beautiful porcelain skin with no freckles and startlingly sapphire blue eyes. Her eyes have an exotic slant, her nose is slightly wide at the end and her lower lip is fuller than the top. Her face is heart-shaped and she is quite dainty, just like I am.

Declan hurries over to me with an eager smile and pulls me into his arms to kiss me soundly.

"This is my sister, Anouk O'Shea. Anouk, this is my girlfriend Journee." Declan introduces us happily. Anouk smiles at me hesitantly and I get a wave of her self-consciousness as well as her fear that I won't like her. I walk right up to her and give her a warm hug.

"Welcome to the family, Anouk," I whisper into her ear. "I'm ecstatic to finally meet you."

When I let her go and look up into her eyes, I see relieved tears that she wipes away with the back of her hand. By this point, everyone else has joined us in the living room so I turn to them with a smile.

"This is Declan's sister, Anouk. Anouk, this is my friend Victoria, my aunt Xanthia, and my guardian James." I introduce everyone.

Anouk smiles bashfully at everyone, so I pull her down on the sofa next to me while I fill Declan in on my visit with Edward.

ANOUK

Victoria, Anouk, and I go up to my bedroom after dinner to watch movies together and get to know each other better. Anouk is more comfortable by this point, and I can see that Declan is thrilled that we are accepting her into our little circle.

"So, tell us about your life in Vegas," Victoria asks Anouk curiously. "Then Journee and I will tell you all about us."

"Well, my mom worked for the brothel there outside of the city, so I was born and raised there with the other kids of the women there," Anouk explains. "My mom died when I was only six years old, so I just stayed there because I didn't know if I had other family or not. The other kids and I went to a local school in the small town nearby where we were all teased because of where we lived. The owner of the brothel, Connor, came when I had just turned fourteen and he told the women he wanted me to start accepting clients. They lied to him and told me I was only ten years old and much too young, so I managed to avoid joining the business."

"That's terrible!" Victoria exclaims. Anouk just shrugs as if this sort of thing is normal.

"Is it true that you are psychic?" Anouk asks me hesitantly.

"Declan told you?" I question with a warm smile and Anouk nods. "Yes. I am an empath and am telepathic as well."

"What is an empath?" Anouk wants to know eagerly, and I smile as I notice that she is really finally starting to relax around Victoria and me.

"I feel what other people around me are feeling," I explain. "I could tell that you were very uncomfortable downstairs when we all first got home."

I can also communicate this way too.' I share with her telepathically. *'In addition to this, I can listen in to people's thoughts.'*

"That is so cool!" Anouk exclaims with a bright smile.

"So, you were never made to work for the brothel?" I ask her anxiously.

"No, the women who raised me refused to let that happen to me," Anouk says with a fond smile. "I guess being exposed to that lifestyle made me really introverted and shy."

"I was always that way at school too," I confess to Anouk. "I felt so different knowing that I was an empath, and the other kids weren't that I just felt uncomfortable. Here, you can start over, and no one needs to know about your life in Vegas."

"I have always wanted to start over," Anouk states thoughtfully. "Declan thought I might want to go to the same school as Victoria, but I'm not Catholic."

"That isn't important," Victoria says with a laugh. "They care more about the money they are paid for tuition."

"Why don't you go there?" Anouk asks me curiously. "Declan said that you are homeschooled now."

"It will be easier for you to understand if I explain my history," I tell her with a smile. "My mom died when I was ten from a fever that was caused by my stepfather poisoning her. I didn't know he killed her until I moved here in November, nor did I know he wasn't my biological father until we moved here either. Ansen, my stepfather, had gotten himself involved in the Irish mob when we lived in Seattle. Connor's death, the head of the Incorporated, was a result of Ansen turning them into the feds so we moved here to New Orleans to hide away from the mob.

Ansen planned on raping me as part of his revenge on my mother for deceiving him into thinking I was his daughter. Unfortunately, he had confessed these plans to Connor which had been recorded. Your brother and I had met right before my mother died and I guess we just connected. Declan promised himself he would protect me, especially after seeing what Ansen was planning on doing to me. Declan knew we had moved here to New Orleans and knew that I was in danger from Victoria's brother, Rafe. Rafe is an empath like me, but he is mentally ill and likes to hurt people.

I stopped going to school because of being in danger from Rafe, Ansen, the other guy at school who was raping girls, and everything else in my life that was happening. I thought I could finish high school sooner if I homeschooled." I finish my story.

"Did your stepfather rape you?" Anouk asks, her eyes wide and frightened.

"No, he did wake me up a couple nights after he had crawled into bed with me whispering my mother's name," I tell her with a shudder.

"Where is he now?" Anouk shivers.

"He is missing." I explain.

"Do you know who your biological father is?" She wants to know.

"Yes. I did a DNA test and found him that way. I actually just met him this afternoon for the first time." I tell her with an excited grin. "He has a thirteen-year-old daughter named Demi, so I have a sister now too."

"Are you going to be living out at Declan's place or here?" Victoria asks her curiously. "Declan is never out there."

"I think Declan already talked to James about staying here. He thought it would be easier for me to adjust if I had another girl in the same house." Anouk says.

"That's great!" I exclaim happily. "I'm so glad that you will be here."

"Are you sure it isn't just because that means Declan won't be going back to his plantation?" Victoria teases, which makes me blush. "Heaven forbid that you sleep without him."

"You and my brother are sleeping together?" Anouk asks obviously shocked.

"Yes," I confess, coloring even further. "I was beaten up by Victoria's brother pretty bad and ended up with broken ribs. Declan was afraid to leave me alone because I might have nightmares and then it was that we couldn't sleep without the other one. We haven't had sex yet so it's not like that."

Victoria insists that I tell Anouk the story of how Declan and I met when we were kids so I go into detail for her. She places her hand over her heart with a sigh when I come to the end of my story.

"That is the sweetest thing I have ever heard!" Anouk exclaims.

The three of us settle down on my bed to watch some movies together for the rest of the night. After Victoria and Anouk have fallen asleep, I make my way down the hallway to the room that Declan is sleeping in and climb into bed with him.

"I was wondering if ye was coming." He pulls me close and kisses me passionately. I return his kiss as I still try to feel something. I have come to the conclusion that there is something wrong with me or passion doesn't really exist. I didn't respond to Rafe either. We were only apart for a couple days but to me, it felt like forever. I fall asleep with my head on his chest and his arms wrapped around me tightly.

The next morning everyone meets in the kitchen pretty early all excited because it is Christmas eve. We sit around the table chatting over coffee about the holidays.

While Dad is making breakfast and Victoria and Anouk are taking showers, I take Luka for a walk because it has been a few days. I put on a pair of leggings and a sweatshirt since it is a little bit chilly outside.

Luka is excitedly marking his territory everywhere and since he seems to be enjoying his walk so much, I add another block just for something different. We are just rounding the farthest corner when a huge great Dane runs past us without a leash or anyone appearing to be with him. Luka is surprised and to my dismay pulls himself free of me to take off running after the large dog. I call him and even try communicating telepathically with him, but he ignores me.

Sighing I take off running after him, deciding to just fetch him myself. I have only made it a few feet when a van pulls up alongside me, the sliding door opens, and I am pulled inside. I am unable to scream out loud as I am being held tightly with a hand over my mouth. Terror freezes me in place, and I fail to call out telepathically to anyone at the house who can help me. I am pushed down onto a mattress in the very back of the van and the man holding me appears above as he pins me beneath him.

Ansen!

Dawn M Williams is an author of paranormal fiction that is full of romance, betrayal, murder mystery, and psychic abilities.

She was raised in West Central Wisconsin and has lived most of her life in Western Michigan along the lakeshore. She shares her home with her supportive husband and her very spoiled pug, Chika.

Her and her husband have four adult children and eight grandchildren. Dawn has a love of history, renaissance and Celtic festivals, rustic camping, Celtic music, and losing herself in the worlds she creates for her readers.

www.ingramcontent.com/pod-product-compliance
Lightning Source LLC
Chambersburg PA
CBHW021027130626
46552CB00005B/1722